THE OTHER SIDE

HEATHER
CAMLOT

Red Deer Press

Published in Canada by Red Deer Press,
195 Allstate Parkway, Markham, ON L3R 4T8

Published in the United States by Red Deer Press,
311 Washington Street, Brighton, MA 02135

Library and Archives Canada Cataloguing in Publication
Title: The other side / by Heather Camlot.
Names: Camlot, Heather, author.
Identifiers: Canadiana 20200181750 | ISBN 9780889956148 (softcover)
Classification: LCC PS8605.A535 O84 2020 | DDC jC813/.6—dc23

Publisher Cataloging-in-Publication Data (U.S.)
Names: Camlot, Heather, author.
Title: The Other Side / by Heather Camlot.
Description: Markham, Ontario : Red Deer Press, 2020. | Summary: "In this poignant coming of age young adult novel a twelve-year-old boy is swept up in the mystery of a young girl's death as he comes to terms with his German grandfather's past during World War Two" -- Provided by publisher.
Identifiers: ISBN 978-0-88995-614-8 (paperback)
Subjects: LCSH: Families -- Juvenile fiction. | Detective and mystery stories. | Bildungsromans . | BISAC: YOUNG ADULT FICTION / General.
Classification: LCC PZ7.C365Oth |DDC [F] – dc23

Red Deer Press acknowledges with thanks the Canada Council for the Arts and the Ontario Arts Council for their support of our publishing program. We acknowledge the financial support of the Government of Canada through the Canada Book Fund (CBF) for our publishing activities.

2 4 6 8 10 9 7 5 3 1

Edited for the Press by Peter Carver
Text and cover design by Tanya Montini
Printed in Canada by Houghton Boston

www.reddeerpress.com

In Memoriam

Elda and Dieter Reppin

For the stories you shared, the son you raised,
and the grandchildren you loved more
than anything in the world.

CHAPTER 1

Saturday, May 31, 2014 – Prince Edward County

"Liiiiiiiam. Where are you?"

I focus on the black and yellow soccer net. Try to ignore Elvy kicking up stones and making the dry moss crackle as she gets closer. I take a deep breath. I am Robert Lewandowski, top scorer in the Bundesliga.

"You need to help me look," my sister says when she wanders out of the woods behind my grandfather's house. The land here by the road is flat and grassy, perfect for playing soccer. By the house, it's all rocky so you can't stake the goal posts into the ground, never mind kick straight. Elvy looks like a windmill, all stick legs and arms, as she cartwheels close to the net, even though she can see I'm getting ready to kick.

I bring my right leg back and release. The ball speeds toward the net. Top left corner. Goal! I raise my arms and high-five my nonexistent teammates.

"Because that's not embarrassing," she says sarcastically.

I drop my arms.

Elvy springs into the net and grabs the ball.

"Mom said we can't go inside until we find everything on the list."

"You really think she's not going to let us in Opa's house if we don't find a snakeskin and a stone with a fossil? Just pass me the ball."

She drops it and boots it my way. She's got a pretty good kick for a nine-year-old, but I don't tell her that because I don't want to play with her. She's whiny, clingy, and annoying. If she thinks I want to play with her, I'll never get rid of her. I roll the ball onto my right foot and go into keep-ups.

"That's what Mom said."

"It's just a way to get us outside and away from screens, you know that, right?" Five, six, seven ... Opa's house is out in the middle of nowhere in Prince Edward County, more than two hours away from Toronto, where we live. When we're here, we're supposed to "explore nature," which is not-so-secret code for hand over phones, tablets, and laptops.

"She said it's a treasure hunt."

"You're so stupid sometimes." Ten, eleven, twelve. I switch to foot, thigh, shoulder, head, shoulder, thigh, foot, reverse.

"Am not!"

Out of the corner of my eye, I can see her stomping over.

"Just go back to your treasure hunt." Foot, thigh, shoulder ...

Her right leg swings toward my face. I close my eyes and jump back. When I open them, the ball is speeding into the net. She really does have a good kick. Too bad she chose gymnastics over soccer. She only plays house league soccer. For "fun." What a waste.

"You know I'm not allowed to go to the lake alone, and that's where the fossils are," she whines while running back to the net to get the ball, her mess of reddish-brown curls bouncing up and down. Way up in the sky, two black V's float with the current: turkey vultures looking for something dead to eat.

"Get Dad to go with you," I say.

"He's doing something. Lots of papers in messy piles."

"Fine. I'll get you the fossil if you leave me alone."

"Really?"

"Yes, really. I need to practice." My development/rep

coach arranged for a special tryout with this elite soccer academy in two months. You've got to get into their program right from the start, otherwise it's pretty impossible. They have the best record in Toronto of players going pro all over the world. I'm going to play for Borussia Dortmund in Germany's Bundesliga one day.

"Thank you, Liam!" Elvy kicks the ball back to me.

I start keep-ups with my left foot.

"Liam," she whines.

I roll my eyes, let the ball fall, and walk to the wooden lake stairs. Black and red danger tape hangs to the ground from the railings. Dad had put the tape up and called a contractor when he found out the stairs weren't in great shape, the bottom few anyway. My grandfather built the stairs, and the house, too. He loves doing the repairs every year.

Loved.

The couple of bad steps is just one reason Elvy isn't allowed down by herself. But we know which steps to skip. The big reason is that Opa's house is on a cliff. A very, very high cliff. I can hear the waves of Lake Ontario crashing against the shore. The rough water isn't good for the cliff, my father will tell you, then he'll launch into a speech about erosion.

"Did you find one?" Elvy yells from halfway up.

"I'm not down yet." The steps are still slick and slimy

from the morning dew. I make the sharp turn onto the rock path and continue to the last set of stairs. "What the hell?"

"You're not allowed to say h-e-l-l!" The wood steps creak as Elvy makes her way down.

I sprint the last five, jumping over the broken one. "Oh crap!"

"You're not allowed to say c-r-a-p!" Elvy yells again.

"Go get Mom and Dad!"

Her steps get louder. "Did you find a fossil?"

"Elvy, up! Not down!"

"A fish skeleton? A fish skeleton would be better than a snakeskin," she says excitedly, totally ignoring me.

"Elvy, do not come down here!" My voice cracks as I try to hold back the nausea making its way up inside me.

"What's that?" Elvy quietly says when she reaches the end of the rock path. "Liam?"

I twist a branch off a tree by the stairs. I take a few quick breaths and a few quick steps toward the shore. My hand trembles as I reach out and poke the body with the branch.

Nothing. Not a sound.

Except for Elvy's ear-splitting scream.

I stand on the cobblestone beach, staring at the waxy figure of the teenage girl. Her blonde hair is matted to her pale face. The caked-on algae looks like veins running along her stiff arms. Her eyes are closed. She looks like a dead Sleeping Beauty, if Sleeping Beauty wore sneakers, black running shorts, and a red tank top with a cougar's face, all ferocious with teeth ready for blood.

My legs wobble as I crouch a few feet away and scoop up a handful of stones, not taking my eyes off the girl. Opa taught me to skip stones right here on this beach. He showed me how to pick the right one—flat and round for the best bounce; how to hold it—with my pointing finger hooked around it; and how to angle it—about twenty degrees—to get the most skips. Opa can skip a stone fifteen times before it slows down and disappears into the lake. *Could* skip a stone fifteen times.

I drop to sitting and hug my knees to try and stop the shivering. Is she what the turkey vultures smelled? Do they eat people? Would they pick her body clean?

I'm still thinking about turkey vultures when Mom and Dad show up. I'm still thinking about turkey vultures when the police show up. Someone stops me from rocking, lifts me up, and carries me back upstairs, back to Opa's house. They lie me down on the sofa, put a blanket on me.

A cop with surgical booties over her shoes fires off question after question to my parents, to Elvy, to me, but I only hear words—"shell-shocked," "rotten step," "cervical spine fracture," "broken neck," "not long"—words washing in and out like the waves over the body. A dead body. The image is lasered into my brain.

Who is she and why is she on Opa's beach? We skip stones on the beach.

"Danger."

"Accident."

"Missing persons."

"Case closed."

"Business card."

More words. Wrong words. How can this be an accident? The cop taps her pen against a notebook over and over, speaks to someone outside the house.

"Are the turkey vultures eating her?" I ask. The pen-tapping stops. Saucer eyes, open mouths on Mom, Dad, Elvy, and the cop.

"No, kid," the pen-tapper says. "We covered her up."

"Oh," I say. "Okay."

My head pounds with more questions. What was she thinking before she died? Was she scared? Wasn't anyone on the lake yesterday to see her? Why did the cop say "accident"? She should know just by looking at her that it can't be an accident, that the girl didn't just break through a rotten step, then fall and break her neck. And why did she go down the stairs anyway? There was danger tape at the top of the steps.

There's got to be more. Sherlock, or one of those other TV detectives I end up watching with my parents when I can't sleep, would know there's more. There's got to be.

Pen-tapping, people talking, cellphones ringing. Mind racing. Questions, questions, questions. I can't stay here. I toss the blanket, drop the skipping stones I seem to be holding, and run to the garage. My legs are still wobbly, my knees want to give out. My hands tremble as I grab my rusty old bicycle, which is lying on the ground because I never put it away. Why put things away when you're just going to need them again? I get a leg over the bike and balance. I pedal over the rocky drive, and bump, bump, bump until I pass the painted No Trespassing sign nailed to a tree and come to the single-lane county road. Smooth. Quiet. Not a car or person in sight.

I pedal as fast as I can, but I can't leave the questions behind. As I round the bend, I hit the brakes.

A chicken. Crossing the road. Why in the world is a chicken crossing the road? I look in the direction it came from. I look in the direction it's going. I have no answers.

I need answers.

CHAPTER 2

Wednesday, June 4 – Toronto

Stay in the present. That's what Coach says. Stay in the present. Focus on the ball. It's with the other team's defense. Defense. Did the blonde girl have any defense? Stop it. Stay in the present. Ball's still in the other half. I've got time. Time to think about the girl. No, the game. How did I not know the last ball was going top corner? Too high. Missed it. Goal. Game tied. We need to beat the Muskrats. Stupid name. Crap team. So why are they doing so well? Now. Then. Alive. Dead. Why? Stay in the present. Where's the ball?

WHACK!

My eyes flutter open. Light blinds me. Sun. The back of my neck tickles. Grass. A hand runs along my cheek. Mom.

When she sees me see her, she leans over, her brown curls hanging over her wide brown eyes, not enough to cover the worry lines between her eyebrows. She's biting her bottom lip. Which means she's trying not to freak out.

"Sweetie, can you hear me?" She brushes imaginary hair off my forehead.

"Mom, you're not allowed on the field."

"Yes, we've told her. Several times," Coach, kneeling on my other side, says grumpily. The ref hovers over Coach, tries to stare down my mother to make her leave. Good luck with that.

"I'm going to take you to the hospital," Mom says.

"Why?"

"The ball hit you in the face and knocked you flat on your back." She feels my forehead, like I can get a fever from being hit by a ball.

"So I stopped the ball?" I lift my head to scan the field, but I don't see the ball. I wonder if it's behind me. In my net. I really hope it's not in my net. I try to look, but Mom won't let me turn my head.

"Yes, you stopped the ball."

"So, game's over, right? A tie. Cool. I can live with that." I crunch up. My teammates and the opposite team are on bended knee. Elvy and the other little brothers and sisters are motionless. Parents in their rainbow of lawn chairs crane their necks. Every last one of them is staring at me. Coach puts a heavy hand on my shoulder before I get any further off the ground.

"I gotta check you," she says.

I don't know what the big deal is. I'm fine.

Coach's long, too-black-to-be-real hair brushes my face and I crinkle my nose from its tickling. She uses her other hand to pull her hair back and twist it out of the way.

"Seriously, I'm good." I try to stand up. Again. I'm held down. Again.

She asks me a long list of questions. When I get them all right, Mom finally moves off the field and Coach lets me move. A round of applause breaks out as I get to my feet.

"You okay?" my friend Ryder asks as we walk to our bags. He's always smiling. I could be hit by a truck or win the World Cup and he'd have that same smile.

"Fine." I grab the ball out of his hands and start keep-ups.

"Seriously?" He tries to take it back, but I'm taller and faster. Parents and players from both teams aren't interested in me anymore and pack up to go home.

"I know your dream is to be Roman Weidenfeller, but you don't actually have to copy his every move," Mom says as Ryder grabs the ball back from me and runs off, his little brother pulling at the back of his oversized red- and yellow-striped jersey.

She's talking about the hit Borussia Dortmund's goalkeeper took to the face a couple of weeks ago against Bayern Munich, their rival in the Bundesliga. Before I was born, my mom couldn't even say Weidenfeller. She learned about soccer because of me and takes me to games. Even though we live in Toronto, she roots for Montreal, where she's from. Dad goes for Toronto, where he's from. Montreal and Toronto are like Dortmund and Bayern, total rivals. Which makes watching games with my parents really fun. Honestly.

"It wasn't that bad. It doesn't even hurt," I tell her. I scan the field for Ryder, now a good thirty feet away and smirking at me as he pops the ball onto his shoulder and lets it roll down his right arm and back onto his right foot. Show off.

"You're twelve and you don't get paid a cent to play. Keep your face out of the game until you make millions. Got it?" Mom says.

"Got it."

Mom starts packing up my stuff. I know I should do it but she is, so why would I bother?

“Collect the balls,” Coach says, tossing me a fluorescent-orange mesh bag.

“But I’m injured.” I give her my best droopy eyes, adding droopy mouth for effect.

“Go now and I won’t make you clean up the blood you left on the field.”

I feel my face for blood, then realize she’s kidding.

She puts on her Bayern baseball hat that I do my best to ignore. She’s a good coach. With bad taste. “You were thinking about the goals that got past you.” Her black eyes narrow, like she’s trying to read my brain.

“No … well, maybe only a little.” Which is true. The rest of the time I was thinking about the dead girl. Someone needs to. The cops think it was an accident. There’s no way. Something about what I saw is messed up—besides a teenage girl being dead on my grandfather’s beach, I mean. The nausea creeps back up. I swallow hard to push it down. It only partially works.

“Liam.” Coach shakes my shoulder with her black-painted nails.

The picture of the dead girl fades. But it’ll come back. It keeps coming back.

“You keep thinking about the past, you’re not going to have a future.”

CHAPTER 3

Thursday, June 5 – Toronto

The school field is looking pretty green. The caretaker is pushing a machine that kind of looks like a lawn mower, paint spraying out to remake the lines for the soccer game we have against another school at the end of the day. I'm on the school team and a development/rep team, the one where I got the ball to the face. Which, by the way, my mother still took me to the hospital for, even though I passed Coach's concussion test. And because of that, we had to watch the end of the second leg of the Canadian Championship between Toronto and Montreal on her phone. At least we caught the one and only goal—by Montreal. That made her worry lines go away, for a few minutes anyway.

The caretaker starts on the goalkeeper's box. An outline. Did the police make an outline for the dead girl, or would the lake have just washed the chalk away?

"Liam," my homeroom teacher, Ms. Guerrero, says. "Please focus. This is important."

I take a last look at the field through the window, push the image of the dead girl to the back of my brain, and check back into the classroom. The salmon-colored walls look exactly the way the room smells. Posters hang everywhere with words and names we're supposed to memorize: *Métis, Colony, Jacques Cartier* ... Everyone looks like they're one head-nod away from their foreheads hitting their desk, it's so hot in here.

"Today, we're going to write thank-you cards for residents at the veterans' hospital." Ms. Guerrero walks down the first row of desks, handing out cards.

"Why?" Ryder asks mid-yawn.

"Because tomorrow is the seventieth anniversary of the D-Day invasion, when Canadian troops landed on Juno Beach on the Normandy coast of France and fought to keep us safe. The least we can do is thank them with a card."

"Can't we just send them a Snap?" Kane asks while trying to balance a pencil on his finger and throwing his head back to get his blond mop of hair out of his eyes.

"You think soldiers who fought in World War Two have Snapchat?" Ms. Guerrero asks, looking unblinkingly over her thick, purple-framed glasses—which is her way of challenging a student to give her an answer that doesn't suck.

"Then we can email them. They must have email," Kane tries again, still balancing the pencil, still flicking his hair.

"We cannot email them." She walks down the next row of desks.

"Why not?"

"Because nobody wants an email to commemorate D-Day."

"I don't think they'd want a card, either. Why would they want to remember a war?"

She stops in front of Kane's desk. "It was a time of brotherhood, of valor, of fighting for what they believed in. They gave their lives to protect their country. They lost friends, family, parts of themselves, but they answered the call of duty and they served proudly."

Kane's cheeks go red as he squirms under Ms. Guerrero's stare. He quickly takes the card she's holding out for him, smiles awkwardly, then starts doodling in his notebook with his pencil.

"Any questions that don't involve trying to weasel out

of work?" Ms. Guerrero asks with a patient smile, her glasses back up on the bridge of her nose.

"Can I send cookies?" Reagan asks, her hand still in the air. "I love baking cookies. Do you think the veterans would like chocolate chip or oatmeal raisin? I think old people like raisins—I know my grandma does. Do you think they have peanut allergies?"

Some kids giggle. Others groan. I roll my eyes.

"That's very sweet, Reagan, but the cards will suffice. I have to drop them off after school."

"But—"

"Just the card." Ms. Guerrero wheels a television to the front of the class and hits play on the DVD player. "First, a documentary about D-Day."

The screen fills with soldiers on some sort of boat, jumping into waist-deep water, struggling their way to a sandy beach on a rough day with the clouds blocking out the sky. Then out of nowhere: Pound! Pound! Pound! Army boots attack that beach like some creep of a kid crushing an ant, kicking up sand as the soldiers run, gunfire blasting, bullets whizzing, shells exploding, faces contorting, bodies hitting the sand. The words "crossfire," "bloody," "rain of death" slice through the soundtrack like the sawing of a jet-ski on a calm, open lake. I look out the window. I see the dead girl on a sandy beach on a rough day with the clouds blocking out the sky. She's staring at me. I stare back, and I know I have to pound, pound, pound out of here.

"Wake up," I scream, but she doesn't wake up. She can't wake up because she's dead on a sandy beach on a rough day with the clouds blocking out the sky.

Kids don't just die for no reason. They don't just die by accident. "Wake up!" I try again.

A gasp. A breath.

They don't belong to the dead girl.

"Liam." Ms. Guerrero shakes my shoulder with one hand and fans my face with a card with the other. Everyone is staring at me. Again. "Liam, you were awfully vocal. Are you okay?"

Everyone keeps asking me if I'm okay. Everyone keeps asking me about the body. Everyone keeps asking me if I want to speak to a therapist. My mom didn't bother asking, she just dragged me to one on the advice of the pen-tapping cop. I didn't say a word the whole time I was there. There was nothing to say. I'm fine.

Anyway, this is all Ms. Guerrero's fault for showing us a stupid documentary with soldiers getting shot on a beach. I snatch the card she's fanning me with.

"Liam," Ms. Guerrero bends down and whispers, "I'm concerned about you. Please let me know if there's anything I can do to help."

"What are we supposed to write on our cards?" Ryder, my best defender, jumps in, deflecting the conversation. I shift my head to see past Ms. Guerrero to nod my thanks. Ryder nods back.

Ms. Guerrero gives me that same pleading look my mom gives me every day, then straightens up, turns to Ryder, and goes back to her regular voice. "Use your imagination. What would you like to say to a war hero?"

I don't have anything I'd like to say to a war hero. I look at Kane, sitting on my right. He's written *Thank you for protecting our country. From Kane*. Real deep.

Alessia, usually on Kane's other side, is already handing in her card when the bell rings. She rummages through her knapsack and puts on a red hoodie with a cougar's face, all ferocious with teeth ready for blood.

Oh crap!

I scribble a note on my card and drop it on Ms. Guerrero's desk so I can catch up to Alessia.

"Liam."

I'm almost out the door when Ms. Guerrero calls me back, her purple glasses down her nose. "I'm not sure this is an appropriate message for a veteran."

"It's the first thing that popped into my head," I say as I keep my focus on Alessia.

"Yes, I'm sure it is. Would you like to re-read it?" She says this more like a statement than a question. She hands me the card.

Why are you dead? From Liam.

She slides a new card across her desk.

"Alessia!" I run down the hall in a shuffle and sprint like we do in soccer warm-ups, trying to get around the crowd of people hanging by their lockers.

"Watch out, Liam, Jesus!" Reagan yells after I shuffle and sprint right into her.

"Sorry!" I yell back over the laughter and locker slams, staying on Alessia's trail. I push through a closing door and catch up to her, but she doesn't look pleased to see me. I don't know why. We're friends, after all. We talk all the time. Her family has a cottage right near Opa's house. She even tried to kidnap Elvy once so she could have her own little sister. I didn't rat her out because I thought it was a good idea. Now Alessia looks at me like I'm some sort of repulsive leech. Real nice.

"Liam—"

"I have to talk to you," I say, taking deep gasps of air. Why am I winded?

"This isn't a good time."

"It's important." I hear giggling, but I stay focused on Alessia. Three inches taller than me. A gazillion black braids. One red sweatshirt.

"Obviously. You followed me into the girls' bathroom."

I un-focus from Alessia and look around. I am definitely standing in the girls' bathroom. With a bunch of girls.

"Yeah. Okay. I'll just ..."

"Wait outside."

"Yeah." I back out quickly and plant myself against the rotten-pumpkin-colored brick wall by the rotten-pumpkin-colored bathroom door.

"Something we should know about you, Liam?" Ryder asks, slamming shut his locker door, dented from one too many soccer balls.

"And if there was?" I ask, tapping my foot impatiently, wishing I had my soccer ball.

"You really know how to ruin a joke," Ryder says through his perma-smile.

"What's it like in there?" Kane asks, his green eyes all wide as his pale face closes in on mine.

"I really didn't notice," I answer, rolling my head to the

side to check the bathroom door. Still closed.

"Nothing?" he frowns, like I need to give him something.

"Um, I guess it smells better."

"I thought so."

Ryder eyes Kane, then looks at me and rolls his eyes. What's taking Alessia so long? What do girls do in there that takes so much longer than guys?

The door finally opens and a stream of giggling girls catwalks out, all in their non-uniform uniform of leggings, sweatshirt, sneakers, and stink eye. Alessia's at the end of the line. She drags her braids behind her back with one hand and puts the other on her hip.

Ryder and Kane make googly eyes and lip-smacking sounds. Alessia stares them down with wicked laser eyes. They head to class, but I can still hear them laughing.

"What's so important that you followed me into the bathroom?" She speaks gently, like the therapist. Blech.

"Where did you get that sweatshirt?" I check out the logo. A soccer ball is clenched in the cougar's teeth. Weird that there isn't any lettering with the name of the team or the town. But I don't need the town. I already know it.

"Are you finished staring at my chest?"

My cheeks get hot. I sink to the floor along the rotten-pumpkin wall and look up at the yellowed acoustic-tile ceiling, only to see Alessia looming over me. I feel like the sand under the soldiers' boots. The bell rings. Sneakers swish and squeak and clop against the beige linoleum floor as the last of the kids in the hallway rush past to get to class.

"She played soccer," I say in the silence.

"Who?"

"The girl." I bite my bottom lip, cup my hands together, and breathe into them to warm them. It's sweltering in school but every inch of me is cold.

"The girl at your grandfather's house?" Alessia says this more like a statement than a question. She knows what I'm saying even when I don't. She slides down the wall to sit beside me. "You know she has a name."

"She does?" I say, staring at the ceiling, at the image of the dead girl floating above me. She's sending the chills. I hug my legs.

"Everyone has a name, Liam, but yeah. It was in the County newspaper. Whole long article about her."

A whole long article? How much could they have to say? Do they know why she was at my grandfather's house? Why she went down the cliff?

Alessia elbows me in the ribs.

"Ow! What did you do that for?" I rub my side. She's got strong elbows.

"I said I'll look for it."

"Look for what?"

"The article, I'll look for the article," she repeats, not annoyed. "Her name was Calynn."

"She was pretty," I say before I know I'm saying it.

Alessia smiles. "The article has a photo of her. She was pretty."

A grunt is followed by a growl and then an "ahem." We follow the black Doc Martens to the brown corduroy skirt to the stiff white shirt to the stiff white face.

"Hello, Principal Cadman," Alessia says, all cheery and professional, like it's okay we're on the floor. "Have you had a chance to read over my proposal?" She pulls out a book from her knapsack and holds it against the cougar's face on her sweatshirt. *The Kids Book of Black Canadian History*. Okaaaay.

Now the principal is staring at Alessia's chest. "Don't you two have some place to be?"

"We certainly do," Alessia says. I make a move to stand up, but Alessia puts a warm hand on my knee.

Principal Cadman moves from staring at the book to staring at us. "I've read your proposal, spoken with our librarian, and sent it along to the board," she says with a twitch.

“Thank you.” Alessia lifts her hand. I guess that’s my cue to move. We slide back up the wall, give a half-smile, and pound, pound, pound to French class.

“What was that about?” I ask, pulling to a dead stop in front of the door.

“Taking a stand.” We walk into class, leaving no one behind.

CHAPTER 4

Friday, June 6 – Toronto

We pull into Sunnybrook Hospital and spend what feels like forever trying to find parking. Around, around, around we go ... Elvy sings in her high-pitched squeal to every pop song on the radio. I want to shoot myself. At least I'm at the hospital.

We park and head to K-wing, the Veterans Centre. We squirt our hands with some sort of disinfectant, walk the long hallway with soldiers, planes, and a woman holding flowers carved into the wall. We turn at the gift shop, then do another long walk, this time to the elevator. We pass a sitting area with cases of military uniforms and medals, and a wall of warplane pictures, which are pretty cool. I like the one called *McKnight's Hat Trick* because it reminds me of soccer, even though this hat trick is about shooting down three enemy planes, not scoring three goals. It's Opa's favorite, too.

Opa's sitting in the hall, outside the small games room that has a pool table and puzzles. He's laughing so hard his face is all red, which with his white beard makes him look like Santa Claus—if Santa Claus wore a green bathrobe. My mom says he looks like Ernest Hemingway, some author who once lived in Toronto and wrote something about a bell.

Opa's got a card in his hand and keeps hitting his knee with it. Elvy tries to climb onto Opa's lap, but Dad lifts her away and puts her on one of the beige airport-lounge-looking chairs beside him. I look around at all the old people in the center. There's a lot of them. A lot of them wearing hospital gowns and sitting in wheelchairs, like my grandfather. Some of them are wearing uniforms with medals and ribbons, military berets with badges on them, which seems weird. Then I remember it's June sixth—the seventieth anniversary of D-Day and the Juno Beach invasion. I don't know what any of the medals or ribbons or badges mean. But the old soldiers smile sadly and salute one another as they roll past in their wheelchairs.

A couple of musicians tune their instruments on a small stage. Feedback thunders through the room, bringing every other noise to a complete silence.

Tap-tap-tap on a microphone. "Sorry about that, folks!" one of the musicians says. The chatter of the veterans and their families starts up again.

"What's got you laughing, *Vati*?" my father asks. Opa, less red now, more yellow, hands him the card. *Thank you for protecting our country. From Kane*. Kane's card. That is funny, but I doubt that's why Opa's laughing.

"Has Opa gone crazy?" Elvy asks no one in particular, which gets Opa and Dad laughing again. I'm glad Dad's laughing. He's been spending almost every hour he's not at work here at the hospital. Would Calynn have lived if she made it to a hospital? Someone would have had to be with her.

"Elvy! Shh ..." Mom says.

Opa wipes his yellowed eyes from laugh-crying, then looks at me with a big old Opa smile. "Do you know why I am laughing, *mein Prinz*?" I shake my head. He leans into us and points to the card. "Because I did not protect our country," he whispers loudly.

"I thought you were in the war!" Elvy says, like she knows which war we're even talking about. The Veterans

Centre has, like, five hundred veterans from World War Two and the Korean War, my father will tell you. Then he'll launch into a speech all about this wing: when and why it was founded, the top doctors who worked here, the new procedures they developed. The fact that it also cares for people who are about to die.

Like Opa.

"I was, *mein kleines Mädchen*. But during World War Two, I fought for Germany, because that's where I was born, that's where I grew up, and that's what I was told to do."

"So shouldn't you be in the hospital there?" she asks.

That makes Opa laugh all over again. "Maybe, my little girl, but I can't go back."

"Why not?" I ask.

The musicians and singer begin the national anthem.

"I'll tell you when you visit next," Opa whispers and winks. "And bring me some glue."

CHAPTER 5

Monday, June 9 – Toronto

On Monday, I tell my friends about Kane's card ending up with my grandfather. We're sitting in small groups because Ms. Guerrero has us creating *Survivor*-like plays about New France that we'll actually have to perform in front of each other. She thinks we'll learn history better if we "live" it instead of just listening to her drone on about it. She's probably right.

"Hey, that's cool!" says Kane. "Did he like it?"

"He laughed," I say, passing my soccer ball from one foot to the other under my desk. I'm in charge of drawing a map of New France. I have no idea how this ended up on me. I can't draw. I open my textbook to the map page and start sketching the shoreline.

"What's he doing at a veterans' hospital if he's not a veteran?" Ryder asks while tapping away on his computer. He insists on making the script look like a script.

"He's still a veteran," Alessia says, making a list of props.

"For the other side. Isn't that unpatriotic or something?"

"He should come visit us in class again," Reagan says.

Opa isn't the kind of person who can sit still, so even though he's been retired from architecture for a thousand years, he was coming to school once a week at the beginning of the school year to help the administration with their design for a new gym building. They loved him so much, Principal Cadman asked him to speak to the students about being an architect, which he happily did. Every time he came, he made sure it paired up with one of my soccer games, school or rep. When he couldn't make it to a game, he'd call afterward to get the play-by-play.

He doesn't call anymore.

I miss the ball. Reagan looks under her desk, butted up against mine, and passes it back. She glances at my drawing and then scrunches up her face, like Elvy does when she doesn't understand something.

"Liam," Reagan whispers, "that's not New France."

I look at my drawing. The shoreline looks like New

France but, moving in, the shore looks more like a cobblestone beach. Opa's cobblestone beach. And on the shore is a body. Calynn's body. I sketched the image seared in my brain. I stare at it, the way Calynn's lying on the shore. Close to the water. Too close to the water. Too far from the steps. How did she get so far?

"You need help, Liam," Reagan whispers again.

I shove the sketch in my knapsack, take a new piece of paper, then restart passes between my feet. "I'm fine," I say.

"So, do you think he'd visit? I can bake him cookies," Reagan says.

"He can't visit."

"Okay. I'll still bake him cookies." Reagan opens her agenda and writes down *Cookies. Liam's grandfather*. I roll my eyes.

"Hey, maybe we can write to him and he can write to us," Kane says. "What do you think, Ms. Guerrero?"

She walks over to our team with an "I know you haven't been working" look, and Kane repeats the idea. She smiles. I guess she doesn't mind because it's related to history.

"I think it is a wonderful opportunity to learn about World War Two from someone who was there," she says. "Would your grandfather be up for answering a question or two, Liam?"

I look at the hopeful faces of my team, all wide-eyed and smiley, as they lean closer and closer to me, like turkey vultures circling their prey. I flash on the body, shudder at the thought of finding her *after* the vultures. Would they have picked her body clean? My stomach churns and I force myself to think of something—anything—else. Soccer. I'm thinking about soccer, the Bundesliga, Borussia Dortmund. Better. I stare at my dorky friends with their dorky expressions.

"I don't know," I say. "Maybe if we can spare some glue."

When I get home after not-talking to the therapist—I'm fine—Alessia is sitting on my porch, reading some novel called *Chasing Freedom.* It's not something we've been assigned, which means she's reading for fun. Who reads for fun? She hands me a laminated page of newspaper without looking up.

I feel the plasticky-ness of the lamination. It squeaks between my fingers. I keep squeaking it—*this* is fun—forcing Alessia to close her book and roll her eyes.

"My dad got a laminator for I have no idea what. He's testing it on everything: parking stubs, movie tickets, scrap paper. Stuff in my room."

"Okaaaay. Why is there even a County paper? Nothing

new ever happens." I glance at the backside of the article listing all the big events of the year: the annual Kiwanis walleye fishing derby, the annual Vicki's Veggies heirloom tomato seedling sale, the annual Geyer coin and stamp show and sale, the annual Mariners' service. Same listings year after year after year after year.

"Obviously new things *do* happen." She flips the page back to the article. "Just read it."

I don't like reading. Too much sitting, not enough moving. And anyway, you can't learn soccer from a book. I look at the photo of Calynn, instead. Her blonde hair is pulled back in a ponytail. Her brown eyes twinkle, but it could be the laminating. I angle the photo a bit to see if anything changes. Nah, they twinkle. And she has a genuine smile, not a fake smile, like the one for the school photographer, or the one for every time someone says I should talk to a therapist.

I read the photo caption: *Calynn Sloan Kearney, age 17, was found dead along the shore of Lake Ontario on May 31. One week earlier she was named* MVP *during a County Cougars soccer game over the Kingston Cormorants.* She's wearing ... no way ... a Dortmund soccer jersey. Geez, we like the same team. Liked. I wonder how she chose it. Even though my grandparents are from Berlin, Dad picked Dortmund for us to cheer for because, for the first three years of house league soccer, I always ended up in a black and yellow uniform, like Dortmund. He said it was destiny. Sometimes destiny makes a right move.

Sometimes it doesn't.

"Who's that?" Elvy yells in my ear. Where did she come from?

"What the hell?" I say.

"You're not supposed to say h-e-l-l."

"You're not supposed to be born." I try to twist away from her, but she stays glued to my back. An engine roars to life, the air buzzing with the sound of our neighbor across the street weed-whacking his patch of grass no bigger than a soccer net.

Elvy sticks her tongue out at me, then looks at the photo again. "Who is she?"

I push her away. She sits on Alessia's lap. Alessia doesn't mind. Ever since the "kidnapping," I've offered her Elvy plenty of times. She just laughs and tells me how lucky I am. She's deluded, but I don't tell her that.

"She's the dead girl," I say.

"I've seen her before."

"Yeah, dead at the beach."

"No, in a car. A teeny tiny yellow car. Remember?"

I flash on a small yellow car. "You mean the one at Opa's birthday party?" I try to remember that day at Opa's house. A month before finding Calynn. A day before Opa's diagnosis. I was playing soccer with Elvy on the grass near the road while all these old people were in the house doing old people things. This yellow car came racing down the road and screeched to a stop at the mailbox across the street. The driver opened the mailbox and a second later zoomed off, but not before the girl in the passenger seat waved.

"Are you sure? I mean, it was so quick, it could have been any blonde girl."

"It was her."

"Did you see the driver?" Alessia asks.

"He had brown hair."

"What was in the mailbox?"

"A letter." She slides off Alessia's lap to do cartwheels on the grass. How is Elvy not bothered by this, by finding a body, by seeing her picture? Like this is normal.

This isn't normal.

Plonk, plonk, plonk.

I look across the street. Our neighbor is dumping the contents of a huge box on his newly weed-whacked lawn with what looks like pieces of a plastic jungle gym. His kids, who are, like, four and five, start picking up the pieces and flinging them at each other. Elvy runs over to play with them, much to the relief of their dad.

Alessia puts down her book and takes the newspaper article, angles it to get rid of the sun's reflection, and re-reads it.

"A 17-year-old teenager who was found along the shore of Lake Ontario on May 31 died from a neck injury after falling down a set of stairs, said an officer with the Prince Edward County Ontario Provincial Police. Calynn Sloan Kearney, a formidable athlete who played soccer for her high school team as well as the all-star County Cougars, was reported missing on May 30 by her parents, Jeff and Mollie Kearney of Picton."

Alessia taps her chin with the lamination. "Picton's almost a half-hour drive. What reason would she have to come anywhere near our places? The Point is so isolated and boring. And how did she even get there?"

"She was wearing running clothes, so maybe she ran," I say.

"I don't think so. That would be like a marathon there and back, even if she was a 'formidable athlete.'"

"If she didn't run, someone must have driven her.

Someone who drove off, because the only car at Opa's when we got there was Opa's."

If someone else was there, that someone could have taken her to the hospital, I think to myself.

"You have to talk to the police," Alessia says.

"About what?" I take the newspaper article back to look at the photo.

"Tell them that she's been to the house before."

"She's been to the *mailbox* before, and what difference does that make?"

"I don't know yet. We need to investigate."

"The police think it's an accident," I say. The police are wrong.

Alessia continues reading the article out loud: *"The body was discovered a day later by the property owner's family visiting from Toronto. Miss Kearney appears to have broken through a rotten step on the stairs down to the lake. The police have not ruled out foul play."*

Foul play, meaning someone else might be involved in Calynn's death. The someone who drove her there and drove off? I scrunch my face at the image of Calynn on the shore. "It only says they haven't ruled it out. They probably say that for everything. When they were at Opa's, I heard them say 'accident.'"

"Yeah, well, your face says foul play." I turn my head to the front door to see my reflection in the glass. Dark eyes, pale skin. I think my face says, You haven't slept in ten days.

She reads more. *"Why she was at the shore is unclear and the police are looking to speak with anyone who may have seen the fall or who had contact with Miss Kearney before the incident. The Coroner's Office said the official cause of death is cervical spine fracture.* It's totally a crime."

"Yeah, well, according to you, the police are investigating."

"And according to you, they're not. Either way, you know something, I can tell. And we're going to figure out what."

CHAPTER 6

Wednesday, June 11 – Toronto

Blood is disgusting.

I know, because it's rushing out of my nose like Niagara Falls. Coach comes running with a wad of Kleenex, pushes it against my nostrils, and pulls my head back. I'm pretty sure it's supposed to be forward, but I can see the look on her face between peaks of tissue, with my head pointed upward and all, and it's not the kind of look you want to cross. The referee rushes us off the field.

"You okay?" Coach asks, replacing the bloody red wad with a new one. I can't see much, but I can hear refs from other games blowing their whistles, coaches calling out plays, parents calling out different plays from the sidelines. The players on my field are on bended knee, waiting for me.

I take over holding the Kleenex, shift it a bit so I can see and talk. "He totally saw me, Coach."

"No one kicks someone in the face on purpose, Liam. He was reckless, but you weren't on the ball."

"I was *literally* on the ball. That's why he kneed me!" Tissue sticks to my tongue. I try to wipe it off with my lips and spit it out.

Our ref taps his watch. "Not much time left. Want to change your keeper?"

"Can you go back in?" Coach asks, checking my eyes for I don't know what.

"Yeah, of course." I take the wad of Kleenex away from my nose. Blood streams out. I quickly push the wad back against my nostrils and pinch.

"Marco, get in there!" Coach calls to my teammate who has never been in net. His eyes go huge and his mouth drops down into the longest opening I've ever seen, wider than when you say, "Aahhh," at the doctor. He looks petrified, like he'd rather be on the bench. Who'd rather be on the bench?

Coach screams out plays. Marco's still wrestling with the goalkeeper gloves when Elvy slides next to me on the bench. At least Mom stayed off the field this time.

"You're supposed to hold your head down, not up, when it's bleeding."

"Thank you, Doctor Elvy. I know."

"You're also supposed to push off to a side and tuck your head a bit when you forward dive." She moves onto the grass to demonstrate: step in, scoop up, push off, smother, kick out. She's pretty good. Such a waste on gymnastics.

"You want to go in net?" I ask as I change wads of tissue again. I don't feel any dripping, so that's good at least.

"Just telling you what you told me." She rolls up to sitting, like a puppy waiting for congratulations on a job well done.

I give in. "You're right, but you better get out of here before Coach catches you."

She sticks out her tongue and runs off.

Marco rolls the ball to Ryder, who takes it up the side and crosses to Arjun, who fakes a shot on net and back-kicks to Kai, who goes for the goal, but hits the crossbar. The same guy who kneed me takes off up the line, weaving in and out, barreling toward Marco. Guess he doesn't know he has teammates. I hate players who think they can do it all. Meanwhile, Marco's just standing there. He doesn't know to bend his knees or have his hands at the ready. He also doesn't know his feet should be no more than ball-width apart, otherwise—

Gah! The ball sails right through his legs. I think I better give him some pointers if he's going to be my backup.

Whistle. Another tie. Crap.

We line up and high-five the other team, then run in for a debriefing. Ryder and Arjun pat me and Marco on the back, but Coach won't have any of it. She rails about missed opportunities, lack of teamwork, and goals that got past us. By "us" she means me, but to cover, she blames our defense as well.

"Practice on Tuesday. And I don't care if you have final tests and assignments. If you don't show up, you don't play." Everyone starts moving, but Coach puts out an arm to stop me.

"Your head is supposed to be in the game, Liam, not your face. That's the second time in a row. I've known you five years and you have never sustained an injury. And now the face? Twice?"

"Coach—"

"I know, Liam," she softens. "I know about the girl and I know about your grandfather. And I'm really sorry. But you are gifted. *Really* gifted. You have to go to that tryout with everything you've got and, right now, you've got nothing." A few more whistles ring out, calling the end of other games. Whoops and cheers and applause fill the air.

"I just need to practice more."

"Your problem isn't skill. It's focus." She puts both hands on my shoulders so I have no choice but to look directly at her face, all heavy black eyes and tight mouth, like someone just died. The awful taste of metal from the blood in my throat turns bitter. "I'm going to play you out next week."

I just died.

"I have the elite tryout in seven weeks. How am I going to get better in goal if I'm not actually in goal?"

"You don't need to get better in goal, you need to get mentally prepared. You're on distraction overload. Your body's reacting to mixed signals—reacting poorly, I might add—and your game is suffering. You've got to sort yourself out. Maybe if you're moving more, your focus on soccer will improve."

The way she says soccer immediately makes me think of Calynn, not soccer. I wonder how her teammates are doing without her. I wonder if she dreamed of going pro. Now she's dead. Whatever dreams she had are dead, too.

"I gotta go," I blurt out. I run past my mother, past Elvy, past Ryder and the rest of the team toward the door, push through the crowd, and jostle my way out. Then I run some more, like I'm second in a race between life and death. I push hard, each step pounding out my anger: soccer, Calynn, Opa, soccer, Calynn, Opa. I pound through the park. Under the trees. Past the dog park, the baseball field, the snack bar. I take a left and head toward the train tracks, not really thinking about where I'm going.

There's a tunnel under the tracks and I end up in a small playground. Kid art hangs along the wood fence—purple and red butterflies, green and orange worms, blue and black flowers. Everything is so easy when you're a kid. When your crappy paintings are considered works of art and your near-saves are rewarded with "You'll get it next time" and a celebratory ice cream, even when your team loses.

I drop onto a swing and feel a slight pain on my right side, just under my ribs. I wonder if Calynn felt any pain. Did she ask the foul-play person for help?

A train rumbles in the distance. Louder and louder. Closer and closer. A whoosh of wind blows against me, but I stay put. I watch the train roll by, the Montreal train I used to call it, because that's the direction it's heading, even if there are hundreds of places between Toronto and Montreal, including the County.

When I was small, my parents used to park the car in a shopping mall parking lot so I could watch the trains from my car seat. We'd just sit and wait and watch. I don't know when I grew out of trains and into soccer, when I traded Thomas the Tank Engine for cleats and shin pads. It just happened.

But things don't just happen. There's a reason.

Trains to soccer because I grew up.

Opa in the hospital because he got sick.

Bloody nose because I got kneed.

Goal to field because I can't focus.

Lack of focus because of Calynn.

Calynn dead because ... because ...

There's a reason. There's got to be a reason. If only she could tell me.

CHAPTER 7

Monday, June 16 – Toronto

Dad comes out of Opa's hospital room and leans against the wall. I shuffle and sprint down the hallway, around the nurses and rolling machines to meet him. We haven't spent much time together since Opa got sick. He's either here or at work, or at Opa's house in the County—but then he's "working" on the repairs Opa never got around to, paying Opa's bills, and doing all sorts of other things and saying he doesn't want any help.

"Are you going to watch the game with us?" I ask hopefully.

His eyes are shiny and red. Usually he shaves his face and his head, but now he's got a scruffy black and white beard and his hair is growing out, making the bald spot

I didn't know he had real obvious. He looks empty, even more than Opa, and Opa's the one with hardly any life left in him. Dad pushes off the wall and gives me a quick squeeze on the shoulder. He doesn't let go. He doesn't speak. Only breathes. Heavily. His weight gets heavier and heavier on my shoulder, like I'm holding him up.

"I have to get to the office," Dad finally says. "And Opa wants to spend some time with you." He gives me one of those sympathetic half-smiles, those "We're in this together" looks, then squeezes my shoulder one last time and walks down the beeping-machine-lined hallway, sidestepping an oncoming gurney.

I plant myself against the wall to let a cheery nurse and her sobbing patient pass, the cries getting louder, not quieter, as they roll away. The horrific sound makes me shiver. When they're gone, I peek into Opa's room: a nurse is replacing his bag of morphine that's supposed to take away the pain. The pain of dying.

While I wait for the nurse to finish, I dig through my knapsack and grab the envelope the kids at school gave me, open it, and pull out their letter. It's typed up, with the date and school address, even a signature line with everyone's signatures at the bottom. Ryder. He obviously insisted on making the letter look like a letter.

Dear Mr. Reimold,

We hope you're feeling well. We're happy you thought Kane's card was funny. Liam thought it would be okay to ask you some questions about World War Two. We hope you don't mind answering.

Why did you fight in the war? Didn't you know you were going to lose? Why would you fight for Hitler? He was such a bad man. How old were you? Didn't Germany learn anything after World War One?

What's it like fighting in a war? Was the food good? Where did you sleep? Did you feel good for protecting your country?

Did you get shot? Was it painful? Were you scared to die? Did you kill anyone? Were you sorry? How many people do you know who died? Would you do it again?

If you loved and fought for Germany, why are you in Canada? How did you get here? Were Canadians nice to you when they found out you're German? Did you ever go back to visit?

Thank you.

Class 7B.

So much for a question or two. It's like everyone asked one question and smooshed them all into one letter. Like they don't think Opa will last long enough for a second letter, or maybe a second answer. The nurse comes out of the room and I head in. I'll let Dad read the letter to Opa the next time he's here.

Opa's two roommates are asleep in their beds, one snoring like a foghorn, the other making this weird gargling noise, but Opa is wide awake and sitting up in bed. He's been here for over a month already. The sun streams through the window onto his face, making him look a little healthier, if you can look healthier when you're dying. The window faces over this garden that's supposed to make people feel better. I suppose if Opa could stand up to see the garden, it might.

"Your mother let you come? I always liked her. A good person," Opa says.

It's lunchtime. I should be at school, but Mom and Dad did the consultation thing and said I could leave mid-day to watch Germany's World Cup game with Opa. He's the biggest soccer fan I know.

"She even drove me." I turn on the television, drowning out the hum of the overhead lighting. Flick. Flick. Flick ... The hospital's got more channels than we have at home. Like patients have nothing better to do than watch TV all day. I guess they don't. They're all just waiting to die. They might as well catch up on all the crap shows. I finally find the game. The whistle blows. Germany versus Portugal. I hunker down in a chair and prop my feet on the corner of Opa's bed.

"We need to talk about Calynn." He says her name like he knows her. God, he knows her. Knew her. Dad shouldn't have told Opa; he's got enough problems.

"Opa, I'm fine."

"Yes, the screaming in school proves that."

Sarcasm. I stare at the television waiting for something, anything to happen to distract Opa from his mission to talk about Calynn.

"Death is hardest for the living, *mein Prinz*, but we must be brave; we must go on living." He's watching me, but I don't turn to make eye contact, just rub my hands together to warm away the chills. "Do you know Irving 'Toots' Meretsky?" he asks.

I have no idea what this Meretsky guy has to do with Calynn, but if it makes Opa stop talking about her, then fine. "No, was he a soccer player?"

"A basketball player. He was the only Canadian athlete at the 1936 Olympic Games who was Jewish, a very brave young man. My father and I were at the opening ceremonies in a stadium much like that one." He juts his chin toward the TV.

I'm so lost in this conversation. "So you saw this Toots Meretsky? That's cool." I glance at Opa. His fluffy white hair has the same bald pattern as Dad. His fluffy white eyebrows are close together as he stares at the TV, like he's trying to find someone he knows in the stadium all the way in Brazil.

"*Nein.*" His eyes get squintier, his nose crinkles, his head lifts off the pillow to get as close a view as possible. "I saw Hitler."

Oh. Oh God. Oh God, oh God. This is worse than talking about Calynn. As a kid with a German father and a Jewish mother, there are things we don't bring up. Did Dad know this is why Opa wanted to spend time with me? Did Mom?

"Opa, we really don't need to talk about the war. Mom said it's hard for people—"

"It's been almost seventy years I haven't talked about it. If I don't talk about the past now, how are you going to change the future? If I don't talk about it now, right now ..." he pauses, like he wants me to fill in the rest. "Then when?"

Opa coughs and I hand him a glass of water from his side table. He chugs it back with a bit of a shaky hand, some of it dribbling down his chin and onto his hospital gown. I open the side-table drawer to look for tissue. It's filled with Popsicle sticks and mini containers of jam and margarine and peanut butter. What in the world is he saving them for? I check the second drawer. It's got a small container of paint and a paintbrush. Okaaaay. I hand him a piece of paper towel and drop in the school glue.

"There were a hundred thousand people in the stadium, and when Hitler announced the games were open, almost everyone saluted." Opa speaks slowly, like when he used to read us picture books. Or maybe like he's watching it all happen again in his head. "I can only imagine what Herr Meretsky thought—felt—at that moment."

"Did you salute?" I let slip. Why did I ask that? Who wants to know if their grandfather saluted Hitler?

"*Mensch*, no. Do you think your parents would have married if I had any respect for Hitler?"

My parents told me they got a lot of strange looks when they started dating after meeting at work, even stranger looks when they got engaged. Like no one could believe it, even though the war was a thousand years ago. My dad makes a joke out of it; he says the German–Jewish thing is easier to deal with than the Toronto–Montreal thing. He's probably right. I've gone to soccer games in Toronto and Montreal with them. That's all-out war.

A thunderous roar takes over the room and, though it's freakishly noisy in here between Mr. Snorer and Mr.

Gargler and my heart pounding from this Hitler talk, the roar is definitely coming from the TV. On the replay, I catch Thomas Müller scoring off a penalty kick, bottom left-hand corner of the net, putting Germany in the lead! I high-five my nonexistent teammates.

Opa smiles but isn't distracted from his mission, whatever that is. "The war had not yet begun, but Germany was still very dangerous. Hitler cleaned up Berlin for the Olympics, took down the 'Jews Not Welcome' signs, told his thugs to stop the attacks during the Games. But if anyone even inquired about the Jewish people, they would be sent to talk with the Gestapo, the Nazi secret police. The Olympics visitors, they would then be closely watched. The rest of us ... anyone who fell into Gestapo custody disappeared forever."

Mr. Snorer, in the bed across from Opa, wakes up and turns on his TV to some movie with a lot of explosions, which is even louder than his snoring and my heart-pounding.

"Herr Meretsky left the athletes village and headed into the city. And he did so alone. My father saw him, watched him knock on certain doors. Those doors opened only so much that a letter could pass through. And that's exactly what Herr Meretsky was doing. He was delivering letters from Jewish families in his hometown who were worried about their families in Berlin. Very brave." Opa takes another shaky sip of water. "Herr Meretsky was doing a favor and wound up in a dangerous situation. Fortunately, it had a happy ending, including a silver medal in basketball."

I sit on my hands to keep them from shaking. I wonder what I would have done. Would I have even gone to the Olympics, to a country that hated me just because I was Jewish, just so I could hopefully win a medal? And if I did go, would I risk letting people know who I was, to help people from home, maybe even disappear?

"Why was your father watching him?" I ask quietly. I need to ask questions, even if I don't want to hear the answers. Because if not now, then when? "What was he doing following a Jewish athlete? How did he even know?"

"He was a very inquisitive man," Opa says, eyes on the TV.

"So, he wasn't, like, Gestapo or anything, on orders to watch Mr. Meretsky?" Why did I ask that? I really don't want to know if my great-grandfather was in the Gestapo. Who would want to know that?

"*Nein, mein Prinz, nein.*" Opa turns his head toward me and smiles his big Opa smile. "My father was religious in his tolerant ways. But that was dangerous, too." The smile disappears. Opa closes his eyes. He's so quiet I think maybe he's ... Oh God. Oh God. I lean over the bed and bring my ear to his face. I feel and hear breathing. Coming. Going. Coming. Going. I sit back down. A tear falls from his right eye and rolls onto his pillow.

"When I was eleven years old, my father was a schoolteacher, and he was teaching our class about adjectives." Opa stares at the television screen again. The cheering is loud, but Opa's quiet voice cuts right through it. "We had to stand up and give an example. Klaus said, Oranges are juicy. Karl said, My brother is mean. Herman said, The English are cowardly. My father, he told Herman that the English were not cowardly, that they were just as brave and worried and upset about the war as everyone else. But he also told Herman that he understood adjectives well and to sit down. Herman was very embarrassed, and he told his father."

My skin goes clammy, giving me goosebumps. I didn't know Opa's father was a schoolteacher. I don't know anything about him. I get the feeling I don't want to know any more. I glance at Opa. He's still looking at the screen. Squinting again. Searching. For Hitler? For words? I look at the television, too, but I'm blind to what's happening.

Opa takes a deep breath. "Herman's father was in the

Gestapo," he says in a slither-whisper, pulling his blanket up to his neck. Oh God. Oh God, oh God.

I walk over to the window and lean my forehead against the pane. The sun streams through the glass, warming me up. The garden below has all sorts of flowers I can't name, massive trees, walking paths, even a small waterfall. I imagine birds are chirping and bees are buzzing out there, but I can't hear them over the noise in the hospital room, over the thoughts in my head.

"What happened to your father?" I say, so quietly I can hardly hear myself. I turn to look at Opa, his now-wide eyes catching, holding mine.

"He disappeared forever."

The final whistle of the soccer game blows. We turn to look at the screen. Four-nothing for Germany. We saw only one goal. On replay.

"Sometimes we only know what is dangerous when it is too late," Opa says in a drowsy whisper. "I wish George and Calynn didn't visit. I wish I didn't ask George to go to the garage."

The garage? The garage is nowhere near the lake. And who's George?

"Opa, why did she go—"

A soft snore fills the air. I close my eyes and sigh.

The most important detail about Calynn, and Opa falls asleep. I'm not going to wake him up, though. Not after that story. He needs his rest. I kiss Opa on the forehead, cross the room in large steps, and slip into the hallway. Calynn, Toots Meretsky, my great-grandfather. All in dangerous situations. Two lost their lives. Meretsky, the one who knew the risks, knew he was stepping into danger, survived. But Calynn's situation shouldn't have been dangerous. She shouldn't have even been there. What favor was this George supposed to do and why did Calynn do it instead?

"Hey, champ." Opa's doctor finds me breathing hard against a wall. He's got huge eyes, tall puffy hair, and suntanned skin. He looks more like a surfer than a doctor. "Not much into hospitals, are you?" That's supposed to be a joke. Supposed to be. Pancreatic cancer isn't funny.

"Is my grandfather going to make it?"

He looks into Opa's room.

"Is my grandfather going to make it till the end of the World Cup?" I figured Doctor Burakgazi would avert his eyes or tell me to talk to my parents. He doesn't.

"You understand what pancreatic cancer is?"

"A death sentence."

"At this stage, pretty much." He smiles sadly. Like

he's happy I understand, but also unhappy I understand. "But there's a good chance he'll make it to the end of the World Cup."

"What about my birthday?"

"When's your birthday?"

"September 1."

"We can hope." He puts his hand on my shoulder, then moves to the next room.

I look at Opa through the open door.

Hope.

I don't have much.

CHAPTER 8

Tuesday, June 17 – Toronto

Alessia is sitting on my porch again when I get home from not-talking to the therapist. I'm fine. This time she's reading *Elijah of Buxton*, also not for school. She's so focused on whatever it's about she doesn't notice me. I tap her side with my foot.

"Ow! What did you do that for?" she asks, rubbing the spot I hardly touched.

"Seemed like the right thing to do." I smile and sit next to her. "What are you doing here?"

"I came to tell you about my investigation." She bookmarks her page and picks up a small notebook, one of those flip ones like you see TV cops use.

"Why are you doing this?" Everyone wants me to stop

thinking about Calynn. Alessia keeps bringing her up.

"Seriously? One, it's boring in the County when you and Elvy aren't there, and this gives me something cool to do." My parents have skipped the last few weekends in the County, said they were too busy to go. Dad is *never* too busy to go. It's practically law that we go every weekend. Went every weekend—until Opa moved to the Veterans Centre. The weekend I found Calynn was the first time we'd gone up since. They think I'll have some sort of freak-out if I'm there. I won't. I'm fine.

"And two, I don't like seeing you sad."

"I'm not sad."

"Upset."

"I'm fine," I mutter.

"Yeah, for sure," she says straight, not a bit of sarcasm in her voice. "But if we figure out what happened to Calynn, you'll be even more fine."

Maybe Opa will be more fine. He's sick and dying and shouldn't be thinking Calynn's death is his fault because he asked for some sort of favor. How can it be his fault? He's more than two hours away from home and can't even get out of bed by himself. And besides, he asked this George guy for a favor, not Calynn. According to Mom, George is an old friend of Opa's from the County—and Calynn's grandfather.

Calynn must have overheard the favor when they were both visiting and decided to do it herself. Or together? But she was at the lake, not the garage. What could Opa want in the garage? I close my eyes to picture the inside but only see Calynn. I gulp some air and bite my bottom lip, feel a hand on my arm.

"I'm fine," I say again.

"I know." She flips through her notebook. "Anyway, I went to your grandfather's house. I wanted to tell you yesterday, but you left school early."

"So what did you find?" I ask, grabbing her notebook. If I can't go, Alessia might as well. She gently removes it from my hands and gives me a new laminated newspaper article instead. Why do I feel like a kid who just got in trouble for playing with their mom's precious new phone? The kids across the street climb their plastic jungle gym and slide down the red slide that's no longer than my leg, shrieking and giggling the whole way.

Elvy shows up with two glasses of water. She hands one to Alessia, looks at me like she's considering whether she should hand the other one over, then sits down on the step and starts sipping.

"I kayaked over to see the cliff, check if anything looks messed up." Alessia turns back to her first page of notes.

"You have, like, a dozen soccer balls stuck up there."

So many soccer balls have gone over the cliff, some managing to skirt the sideways-growing trees and dribble all the way down the rock face, hitting just the right marks to land on the beach. Goal! But others are stuck behind fallen trunks or between rocks and will stay there for all eternity because we're not allowed to climb the cliff—erosion and all that. A graveyard of soccer balls.

"What did you find about Calynn?" I ask. Elvy moves off the porch and goes to work on handstands.

"Right, so I beached the kayak and walked along the shore to work the scene." She flips a page and waits until the kids stop their supersonic squealing to talk. "Then I checked out the broken step."

"So, you could just walk around? No police tape or any of that stuff they use to secure a scene?" *Sherlock* and all the other detective shows have me sounding like a cop, but TV cops react to a dead body all wrong. There's nothing cool about finding a dead body. It's gut-wrenching, stomach-turning awfulness.

"None of that stuff. And the whole last set of stairs, with the broken step, has been replaced. I walked up, looked for traces of fabric, shoe prints, drag marks, vomit, feces ..."

"Ew!" Elvy and I say at the same time.

"It's basic physical evidence. I read that perps always leave traces of themselves at the scene of a crime."

"And you think a possible perp—even though the cops said it was an accident—would take the time to take a dump?" I say this more like a statement than a question. Elvy does flip after flip after flip.

Alessia shrugs. "I don't know how a perp thinks."

"Good to know."

"Ha, ha. Then, I checked the house and garage for signs of forced entry." The little kids walk up the slide and laugh like it's the craziest thing ever. "And then just looked around for anything curious on the ground that might be a clue."

"Like more vomit and feces?" I ask, the sarcasm thick.

"Maybe," she smiles, making me smile, too. She's so weird. "I spoke to the guy who fixed the steps. Works with his dad after school and on weekends. They were just packing up. He said the cops took the broken set of steps." So the contractor finally showed up. But too late. Alessia holds out her phone. "Here, I have photos of everything."

"You mean photos of nothing?"

Whatever was in the garage must have been important if Opa couldn't get it in Toronto. If Calynn died for it. I scroll through the photos: cliff, stones, trees, lake, soccer balls, black pick-up truck, *Geyer and Son Repairs* lettering, repair-guy smiling, driveway, driveway, driveway, garage lock, door lock. Nothing, nothing, nothing.

"Is that a fish skeleton?" I ask as I come to the last picture.

"Yeah, pretty cool, eh?"

"I want to see that!" Elvy runs over and grabs the phone.

"So we're no further than we were before your investigation." I lean back on the step and look up at the sky. No clouds, no planes, no turkey vultures. More nothing.

"I guess not." She takes a sip of her water.

"Hey ..." Elvy says, no longer scrolling through the photos. "That's the guy from the teeny tiny yellow car."

CHAPTER 9

Wednesday, June 18 – Toronto

I run onto the field late, my bag thumping against my back, my Dortmund hat bouncing on my head, my feet tripping over my ball, my stomach feeling like it's going to explode. Not good. Not good at all. I was reading Alessia's latest laminated article in the car, which made me sick. Not the words, the reading in the car. Just one more reason not to read. Mom rushed me out, but I keep repeating the lines in my head.

A local man has been brought in for questioning by the Prince Edward County detachment of the Ontario Provincial Police in reference to the death of Calynn Kearney. The motive surrounding the incident remains under investigation. Police say more information is forthcoming, but the names of possible suspects remain confidential.

Possible suspects. There are possible suspects. Someone drove Calynn to Opa's. George? A grandfather wouldn't leave his granddaughter to die on the shore of his friend's house. Someone else. The local man? Is he a possible suspect?

"Honored by your presence, Mr. Reimold," Coach says with a smirk shadowed by her Bayern baseball hat. Blech. When she sees me grimace while looking at her head, she stands still, with her hands on her hips, like she's daring me to take the hat from her. I don't even want to touch it.

I drop my stuff and join the passing drills. Marco's back in goal. I blast the ball—and my anger—at Ryder, striking him in the gut.

"Jesus, keep it for the game, Liam," he says, bent over.

"Sorry." I try to keep from laughing, until Ryder starts laughing, too. Makes me feel a bit better. A bit.

"Hey, you wanna both be benched?" Coach yells from the sidelines. "Get in here and get dressed proper." We strip off our track suits and jog in place while Coach runs off our positions and plays. I glance at the net and then run to center-mid. Center-mid. I'm really not playing goal.

The whistle blows and Arjun easily takes the ball off

the Vipers forward, a lumbering mammoth who can knock you down just by looking at you, he's that big and scary. Except to Arjun, who's not scared of anyone. Which is good, because that forward is after him as he shuffles up, up, up and passes back to Ryder, but the ball is blocked by their mid. It was a nice try. The guy taps it over to his fellow center, who barrels toward me. I slide my leg just before he reaches me, get the ball, run, run, run, like I'm second in a race between life and death, and pass through a defense's legs to Kai. Finish it ... finish it ... Kai misses the shot.

"Liam out. Xavion in." I look at the clock at the far end of the field. Ten minutes. I've played all of ten minutes before getting pulled. What the hell? Never in my life have I been called off the field in the middle of a game, except when I was still playing house league and we had to take turns, even when no one else wanted to play in net.

I watch as Marco jumps to stop a top-left corner. He spreads his fingers as far as they can go, then swats his hand down with all his might to keep the ball from crossing the line. He's got the height and makes the save. Even he looks amazed. With each minute, Marco looks more confident in goal. The next shot comes out of nowhere and goes straight for bottom right. *Dive! You have to dive!* I scream to myself, but Marco just bends over. What kind of tactic is that? You can't stop a shot like that by bending over. The other team starts cheering and high-fiving.

Their coach changes a couple of players and I look to Coach to do the same. Nothing. After five minutes, I stand by Coach on the sideline.

After another five, I make conversation. I'm the only one talking.

Another five passes and the whistle blows. She finally speaks. "Bring it in, boys!" The score is sitting at one-nothing for the other team. Everyone grabs water and gathers around Coach. She lists everything we've been doing wrong and nothing we've been doing right. Except for Marco. She congratulates him on the save and tells him the grounder was tricky. Um ... no, it wasn't. It was on the ground. And it was obvious the Viper was going to kick it to the right. When the referee blows the whistle, Coach quickly lists off positions and plays. I'm not on that list.

"Um ... Coach, am I going back in?"

"Not yet." She answers without a glance in my direction. Ryder looks at me questioningly and I just shrug my shoulders. The other team is definitely bigger than us, and they have some great footwork and coordination.

Perfect triangle formation for passing the ball all the way up through our guys to the goal. Another kick by their forward and it's looking like it may hit the left-hand goal post. Marco smiles—before realizing that the ball flies off the goal post at an angle that shoots it top right. The other side starts cheering again. Our team yells at Marco, who asks to come off. Coach says no.

With ten minutes left in the game and the score now a pathetic five-nothing, I ask Coach if I can go in again. Our defense needs relief. I need to move.

"Not yet."

"Am I going in at all? Because it seems to me that you'd rather lose than let me play." She wants me to play field to get my focus back, but she's not actually playing me on the field. How's that supposed to work?

"Sit down. You're off."

"Yeah, obviously." I don't get it. I don't know what I've done. Well, I haven't done anything because I've hardly played. I'm glad it's just Mom and Elvy here and not Opa. I wouldn't be able to face him. A player but not playing. I can hardly face him now. Alive but not living.

"Go. Sit. Down." I do as I'm told, my heart sick, and watch as Ryder manages to nab Marco's short throw, making one Viper very unhappy. He passes up to Kai, who moves into the penalty box. Next thing, Kai is on the ground, tripped on purpose by another Viper. The Viper's pretending to check if he's okay, then butts Kai in the head—just like Pepe did to Müller in the Germany–Portugal game I didn't watch with Opa but caught during the highlights later that night. What the hell? The ref doesn't give Pepe junior a red card and kick him off the field, just a yellow warning. That's insane. He does give Kai a penalty kick though. Kai sets up the ball, jumps in place to loosen up, then gives it everything he's got. It's not enough for a goal.

I scan the crowd for my mother, who has that concerned biting-her-bottom-lip thing going on. I nod an *I'm okay* to her and she nods back with a half-smile, like she's hurting as much as I am. Maybe she is, but I doubt it. She's not the one who's been benched. She's not the one with the beaten pride. She's not the one with the matted hair. She's not the one with the caked-on seaweed. She's not the one with the vacant eyes. She's not the one lying dead on—

The whistle blows. Game over. Seven-nothing.

"It's okay, boys, they're a tough team. We'll get them next time," Coach says.

"Yeah, if Liam goes back in net," Ryder says under his breath, but loud enough for everyone to hear. And I mean everyone.

"Five laps, Ryder. And if you talk back again, I'll make it ten." He doesn't bother arguing. Coach goes into her long spiel about the game I didn't play in. I click the cap of my water bottle, each click another question. Who is this stair-fixer guy? Click. How does he know Calynn? Click. What does he know about Calynn's fall? Click. When are we going back to Opa's house? Click. Who are the suspects? Click.

"Liam." Coach is sitting on the bench next to me with her baseball hat on her head. I look around the field. Everyone's packing up and heading out. Elvy and the other little sisters and brothers are running around, picking up soccer balls. Crap. "You zoned out. Again."

"Well, there's not much to do on the bench, Coach," I say with a mix of sarcasm and seriousness.

"An invested player will be analyzing the game, whether he's on the field or on the bench. Ready for the next move. The next play. The next moment he's on. He watches and learns the strategy the other coach is playing, learns which players are trying to pull what, so that when he goes in, he knows what he has to do, who he has to stay away from and where he's going to pass. Especially important for a goalkeeper."

Was someone trying to pull something on Calynn?

Was she trying to stay away from that someone? Who is that someone? It can't be her grandfather. The local man? Did that local man see the fall? Watch and learn. That's good advice.

"Fix yourself. I don't care what it takes, but you figure it out and come back next week and show me you are the player the elite team is expecting to see."

Opa made me the player the elite team is expecting to see. Coach is good, but Opa was my real coach. He used to take notes at my games, and we'd go over them, tactics, techniques—you name it. He'd set up the net on his grassy field in the County every weekend my family went to visit, and he and I would play and train and have fun. He wasn't pushy about it or anything. I pushed myself.

But it's not the same without Opa.

"Liam," Coach's voice softens. "I will help you any way I can, but you've gotta ask. I can't read minds. Any questions right now?"

"Why are you wearing that hat?" I give it a quick glance. There's gotta be a thousand teams in the world and she picks Bayern. Blech.

She laughs, then goes all serious. "Because I know how much you hate it. *But* you've learned to accept it. You aren't consumed by it anymore, trying to steal it from me like you used to when you were a young brat." She smiles and waits for me to do the same. I do. A little. "Now you roll your eyes and move on. I know you're dealing with a lot, but you need to get your act together and take care of yourself. You need to get back in the game."

I need to take care of Calynn. She's not going to just magically disappear from my head, not when so much is still not known. I get what Coach is saying, though. I do. It's like Opa said: *Death is hardest for the living, but we must be brave. We must go on living.*

"Yeah, okay, Coach." I smile. Bigger. Opa would want me to focus on the tryout. That's what I need to do.

She pats my knee. "I also wear the hat because Bayern's far better than Dortmund!" She laugh-grunts, then heads off to the gear bags before I can steal the hat from her and get rid of it, once and for all.

"Why weren't you in net?" Elvy asks in a whiny high-pitched voice as she runs up to me.

"I don't know."

"How can you not know?" she yells as I walk toward my mother.

"Should I talk to your coach?" she asks, biting her bottom lip.

"God, no. It's just tough love. Let's go." I put my

Dortmund baseball hat on my head as Mom takes my bag and calls out to Elvy, who leaps and backflips and cartwheels like a professional gymnast. I look back at the field and at Coach. She sees me. I know she does.

She turns her back.

CHAPTER 10

Thursday, June 19 – Toronto

"Did your grandfather read the letter?" Kane asks as we hit the one-hundred-meter mark on the school track.

"Yeah, has he written back yet? It's been three days," Ryder asks as he catches up then passes us.

"Do you think we upset him? We didn't want to upset him," Kane says, whipping his hair out of his face.

Ryder drops back. "Has he said anything about it?" he asks, then speeds back up.

Geez, I feel like a suspect under interrogation. Suspects. Who are the suspects? I speed up, my feet pounding the ground as the track bends, forcing my heart to beat faster, my breath to get shorter, my sweat to bead bigger. Life is pumping through my veins, life that Calynn no longer has, that Opa soon won't have. I push myself faster. Faster. Faster.

As I round the next bend, our gym teacher, Mr. Liu, waves me down. I slow my pace until I'm jogging, then walking, then keeling over. No one else is on the track. They're all just standing around, some snickering, some clapping. Mr. Liu holds out a water bottle and a towel.

"I think we need to talk about joining the track team next year," he says with a quick, nervous laugh.

I take the water bottle and towel, jog to the locker room, and toss on a pair of track pants. Kane passes me my knapsack. Ryder pats me on the back. Neither says a word as the bell rings, and we run up two flights of stairs to history class, my legs ready to give out. We're late.

Ms. Guerrero is standing at the door. We offer innocent smiles. She doesn't smile back. Her black eyes stare us down over her purple-framed glasses. I hand her an envelope. She opens it and scans quickly, then lets us pass. Canadian history, here we come.

"All right everyone, pencils down please," Ms. Guerrero says. Instead of pencils dropping, I hear last-minute scrapings across paper, kids still filling out their answers to the history test, frustrated sighs from different parts of the room, and one head hitting a desk. I think I did okay. I don't really care. I have bigger worries: Soccer. Opa. The World Cup. Calynn.

New France and British North America? Not so much.

"Pass the tests forward, please. Reagan, please collect them," Ms. Guerrero instructs as she leans against her desk. "Thank you. Now, we have five minutes left of class and I thought we'd turn to *world* history."

Groans all around. She pulls out the letter I gave her and slides up her reading glasses.

"Dear Class 7B,

"You have sent along a wonderful list of questions, and you should be very proud about being so curious and wanting to know about the past. The more we know, even if it is just as hard to hear as to tell, the less likely we are to repeat terrible mistakes. Only by understanding and thinking about the past can we have a future.

"I was almost five years old when Hitler began to rule Germany and eleven years old when Hitler started the Second World War. I was sent to the army when I was only sixteen. Germany was losing and anyone old enough was called for duty. I was told to fight for my country. That is the reason why most people fight. I believed, like everyone else who fights, that we would win. Germany learned a terrible lesson, but not enough.

"War is like nothing you have ever experienced in your life and I hope you never will. You sleep in a tent if you are lucky, or on the battlefield in a dugout. You get something to eat when you are hungry, and something to drink to still your thirst, but you feel good because you do it to protect your country.

"When you fight, you think nothing will happen to you. But that's a lie we tell ourselves. I did not get shot, but I saw others who did. And they hurt terribly. So I was careful not to get in the line of fire. My buddies and I were all scared and afraid to die. I do not know if I killed anybody but would be very sorry if I did. Many people, young boys out of my school, got killed. I hope you and your friends will never have to fight in a war.

"After the war, I worked different jobs to earn enough money to buy a ticket for Canada. I traveled on a huge boat filled with people just like me and made some new friends. I am here because I heard so much about Canada. That Canada is such a beautiful, vast country, full of big lakes and forests and nice, brave people. Canadians always made me feel welcome and at home and helped me. They did not care where I came from. I never went back to Germany. I have long missed my friends I had left behind, my brother, and my mother, who of course missed me. Luckily, she was able to move to Canada, too, but only when she was very old and East Germany would allow her to leave. I never regretted coming to Canada, and here I have lived a very happy life with my family.

"Never stop asking questions.

"Your friend, Friedrich Reimold."

The bell rings. Class is over. No one moves.

"That was some letter," Alessia says, catching up to me in the back of the school. She's got another new book in her hands, a biography of Drake. Seriously?

"Yeah," I say, playing with my soccer ball: foot, thigh, shoulder, head ...

"Did you know any of that stuff?"

I feel her watching me, but I keep my focus on the ball. See, I can focus.

"Not really." Left foot, right foot, left foot, right foot ...

"I thought his story was pretty spectacular."

I let the ball drop and stare at Alessia. "Spectacular?" I spit it as I say it. My eyes narrow and I thrash the ball across the soccer field.

“Hey!” some kid yells after it strikes him in the back. He kicks it back. It rolls slowly. Weakling.

Alessia waits, eyebrows raised.

“He said he fought for Germany because he thought they’d win. What the hell is that? If they had won, what would have happened to the rest of the Jews? To the rest of the world?” I think about Toots Meretsky, risking his life to play in the Olympics, to deliver letters. Bravery over safety. My grandfather fought for Germany rather than help the Jewish people, rather than speak out against the Nazis like his own father did. Safety over bravery. How could he agree to fight for the man who took his father away?

“I don’t buy it,” I say.

Alessia drops her book on her knapsack, takes the soccer ball, and sits on it. She grabs my hand and drags me down to the grass. “He said he was told to fight for his country. He was sixteen, Liam.” She sees the letter poking out of the front pocket of my bag and pulls it out. Reads it again. At the beginning, the handwriting is all shaky. It gets better for a couple of lines, then shaky again. Then it changes completely. Dad’s writing. Which is pretty awful, too, but at least it’s readable.

“He could have chosen to fight with the Resistance. He could have stood up against the Nazis. Instead, my grandfather had a hand in killing six million Jews, Alessia. My mom's Jewish. *I'm* Jewish." I rip a handful of grass from the field and start shredding it. Obviously, I've known for a long time that Opa fought in the war; this wasn't news. But the letter, it's different now. It's made things real. Things I never wanted to think about. Things we weren't supposed to talk about. Why did I agree to the letter?

My grandfather was a German soldier. I have a Jewish family. Did they meet? Did he unknowingly—or worse yet, knowingly?—send my family to their deaths?

"Your grandfather wasn't a Nazi, Liam. Jesus. He was a soldier. A kid soldier."

"And you're trying to make that okay?" I say, ripping out another handful. "What's the difference what kind of soldier he was?"

She makes a sour face but continues. "There's a big difference. He was fighting to protect his country, not to kill your ancestors. Not every German was a Nazi."

"How would you know?" I spit out.

"Seriously? Have you ever actually looked at me before, I mean beyond staring at a soccer team logo on my chest?"

I look at her now and shrug. "You look like my friend, Alessia."

She smiles, like I said the right thing. Then she punches me in the shoulder.

"Ow! What did you do that for?" I rub the pain and look across the field at Ryder and Kane playing catch. Ryder can't catch.

"You just proved my point. I know not every German was a Nazi because I know not every white person is a racist."

I scrunch up my face, no clue what she's talking about. She rolls her eyes.

"Do you know how many books with black characters, about black people, by black authors are in the school library?"

"You think I've been in the school library?"

She rolls her eyes again. "Let's try this: Do you know how many times I've heard the n-word in the halls, like it's okay?"

Oh. That's what she's talking about. I don't know if she's comparing apples to apples, as my dad would say, but I get it. I've heard it. All sorts of crap names for whatever you are, Chinese, Italian, Indigenous, Jewish, Black, the list goes on. I just always shrugged it off.

"I gave Principal Cadman a list of books that should be on our all-white curriculum, in our all-white library."

That's what she meant by taking a stand. That's good and all, but I don't see what that's got to do with Opa. He didn't take a stand. He fought for Germany.

"He believed they would win," Alessia says, folding up the letter and putting it back in my bag.

"Everyone believes they're going to win." I rip out another handful of grass as the bell rings.

Alessia stands up, grabs her stuff, and gives me a hand up. We walk quietly, slowly, to class, me tapping my soccer ball, as everyone else bolts past in a blur. I don't feel any better, but I feel a bit calmer. A bit.

"Hey, Alessia," I say, taking a look at her book. "You know Drake's Jewish, right?"

CHAPTER 11

Friday, June 20 – Toronto

I'm sitting on the school steps, waiting for my mom to pick me up. We had our last school soccer game this afternoon and I'm exhausted. Not because of the game—the other school's team sucks and we whipped them nine-one—but because all I did last night was toss and turn.

When I did actually fall asleep, I had nightmares. I kept thinking about Opa's letter, kept seeing my grandfather as a soldier, like the ones in that stupid documentary we watched in class, uniform from head to toe, a machine gun in his hands.

Bratatatata!

Tossed grenades.

Booming explosions.

Then a scream, a woman's scream.

Calynn falling onto the sandy beach, breaking her neck. Every time I fell back asleep, the same scene, over and over and over again. Gunfire. Grenades. Explosions. Screams. Death.

Mom pulls in along the sidewalk. I hustle over, my ball under one arm, my bag over the other. As I slip into the car, I tell her I don't want to hear any more of Opa's stories—out loud or written down.

"One day you'll be happy he's shared so much with you." She turns down the radio and pulls back onto the road.

"I don't like what he's telling me. I don't—" I stop myself before saying I don't like my grandfather. I love my grandfather but, right now, the stories, the letter. I clench my fists, my nails digging into my palms. I don't like who he was. I don't want to hear any more.

"You don't have to like what he says, but he wants you to know," she says, like she can read my mind. "To understand."

Why would he want me to know? Why would he want me to be angry with him right before he dies? He must know that telling me all of this—*to change the future*—is changing the present. Not in a good way. I just want to go back to liking my grandfather.

"I suspect he's filled with grief or shame or guilt," she

continues. "The past is important, Liam. We must never forget."

"Didn't you forget? You married Dad." I watch the people on the sidewalk—jogging, pushing strollers, walking dogs—through my window. So many people. How many of them think about the past? How many of them consider the past before making a decision about the present, the future?

"Actually, marrying your dad made me much more conscious and protective of my Jewish identity. Honestly, Liam, I was scared to meet your grandfather. I was waiting for him to say something anti-Semitic or horrifying or, I don't know, some slip that would tell me he hated me for being me. I always replayed in my head what I would say to him when that time came. But it never came, Liam. It's been fifteen years of nothing but kindness."

"Or a cover-up."

I think of the movies I've seen about Nazis who snuck out of Germany, who changed their names and their accents, and went on with their lives. Some of them have been tracked down and punished. Some haven't. They could be anywhere.

"Oh, sweetheart, I don't think so. But marrying your dad did make me very determined that you and Elvy understand your Jewish identity, too. That's why you're having a bar mitzvah."

I roll my eyes. More reading. "But Opa could have, like, killed your family."

"No, no. Zaidie's family came from Russia, something like thirty years before the war, and Bubbie's, fifty years before. We didn't have any relatives in Europe at that time, and we don't have any Holocaust stories in our family. If we did, as kind as Opa is, I doubt I would have ever dated your father, much less married him."

"We must have had family who fought in the war." We drive down into the forested valley, cyclists, joggers, waiting to cross the road to the trail. How many of them had family in the war? Lost family in the war? How many of them are angry with their father, their grandfather, for fighting in the war, for fighting on the other side? I clench and unclench my fists. Mash my lips together, hear the little muscles or nerves—or whatever they are—crunch as they roll over my teeth. That actually hurts. A lot.

"Yes, Bubbie's father, but he was stationed in the Bahamas to protect the Duke of Windsor. He said his mother told him to get as far away from the fighting as possible, so he did."

"I didn't know you could choose where to go."

"I'm pretty sure he was joking."

Out of the valley, up to a street full of shops. More people. So many people shopping, talking, laughing, living. While so many others are dying. Are dead. "Why would he joke about war?"

"That's how Jewish people have stayed alive for thousands of years."

"I don't get it."

"Jewish humor. It's a thing." She sees the quizzical look on my face and turns off the radio. "If you don't laugh, you cry. It also helps us to remember: *A lesson taught with humor is a lesson retained*. That's from the Talmud. Don't ask me how I know that."

"Maybe someone was joking when they said it," I say quietly, making Mom laugh.

She pulls off into a parking spot on a sideroad and cuts the engine. She runs her hand along my cheek and musses up my hair. "When did you get so mature?" she says, getting out of the car. "Come on."

We walk a block and I see The Bagel House, the only place Mom will buy bagels in Toronto—the only place, she says, where they taste like they could be from Montreal. Dad calls her a bagel snob. But I'm with her on this one. We go in and she orders two dozen bagels, a chocolate milk, and a Diet Coke. It's hot in here from the wood-burning oven, as hot as the bagels she pulls out of the paper bags, sesame for me, poppy for her. We sit at one of the handful of tables and break our bagels in half.

"I understand it's hard to hear what Opa's telling you, but he wants to share this part of his life before he can't share it anymore."

"But he knows we're Jewish. He knows the Nazis would have killed us."

Mom puts her hand over her mouth and coughs, I'm guessing to dislodge the piece of bagel she choked on. I look at the table, play with the seeds that fell off our bagels. Like one of those Zen garden things. Except it isn't filling me with Zen, whatever that means.

She coughs again and I can actually hear her swallow. "Maybe that's why this is so important to him. He loves you."

"He could have joined the Resistance," I mutter, what I told Alessia.

"Maybe. You'd have to ask him." She pops another, smaller piece of bagel into her mouth.

"Do you know people whose families were killed by the Nazis?" I ask quietly as I pick at the seeds on my bagel.

"Yes. And I know people who are the children of survivors."

"Do I know them?"

"Yes."

"Who?" I ask, but I don't know if I really want an answer. I don't want to be awake all night, seeing my grandfather gunning them down.

CHAPTER 12

Saturday, June 21 – Toronto

"It's Saturday, is it not? I thought you would be at my house." Opa gives me a big old smile. He tries to sit up, but only manages to muss up the sheets and blankets on his bed. I clench my fists and release, then reluctantly straighten things out and make him more comfortable with a pillow. He hits the switch on the bed that makes his top half move up.

"We're leaving right after the game." Dad's desperate to go to the County. I don't know if it's so much to be at Opa's house as to be away from reality. I mean, why else would he leave Toronto, leave Opa? Doesn't really matter anyway. I need to get back so I can investigate for myself.

"Missing precious hours in the County? I must be dying

for such allowances," he says. I catch his wicked grin. It looks more wicked than grin now. He looks different. I don't mean the fact that he's paler and thinner and weaker. I see him differently ... inside. And I don't like what I see.

"That's not funny."

"It's life, *mein Prinz*. Getting old is for the birds." His tone goes serious. So does the look on his face. "How are you feeling?"

He wants to know whether I'm over Calynn. I want to know why he really fought in the German army. I clench my fists and release.

"I'm fine." I pick up the remote from the side table and flick for the game. "Germany versus Ghana today." I keep the remote in case we have to compete with sci-fi explosions or blaring musical numbers or Western gunfights, or whatever Mr. Snorer picks to watch today at the exact same time as the game.

"Ah, the Boateng brothers!" Opa claps his hands together excitedly, making me half-smile. The Boateng brothers are from Berlin like Opa. Except they're playing against each other in the World Cup, because one brother decided to get his Ghanaian citizenship and rep their dad's country. "Sibling rivalry in front of millions of viewers. Not an easy thing."

"Oh, it's easy. I speak from experience," I say.

"You and Elvy have much in common. One day you and she will need each other. And you will be there for each other." He says this like an order. He's not exactly in the position to give orders. We're not in the army.

I bite my bottom lip, try to focus on the game, but keep getting distracted by all the clashing and clanging metal from Mr. Snorer's TV.

"Family is all we have in this world. It's very important to keep in touch, even if you live in different places," Opa says. "I wish I had as long a relationship with my brother as you and Elvy will surely have." Another story coming. I prop my feet up on the bed and squeeze the remote tightly. I don't want to hear it, but what choice do I have? Choice. Don't we all have choices?

"Werner and I were always together until we were not. He was drafted at eighteen and spent the war on a U-boat, a German submarine. Tens of thousands of crewmen perished, but Werner returned home. Of course, we were all starving by then. The country was starving."

So what if the country was starving after everything the Nazis did? Lots of people starved, *were starved*—to death—all because Hitler was a lunatic and nobody stopped him. I want to ask questions, but I don't. We're not supposed to talk about this. Doesn't he understand I'm stuck in the middle, German and Jewish, Jewish and German? What does that even make me? I stare at the TV screen, bite my tongue, and say nothing.

"After the war, Werner and I scavenged the fields and picked up seeds left behind by the farmers after harvest. By winter, the fields were empty and we lived off brewer's yeast. Yeast and seeds—they were treasures."

And all the treasures the Nazis stole? Art, jewelry, gold fillings from teeth. I clench my toes and bite my bottom lip.

"I wanted nothing more to do with Germany. It stole my childhood and sent me to war. Then, when the country was divided, East Germany wanted to steal my adulthood and send me to the uranium mines. Life felt no different than before and during the war. It was peacetime with weapons, goose-stepping soldiers, and the secret police and neighbors spying. I was not prepared to risk death twice. So I escaped."

Wait, what? He didn't talk about escaping in his letter. "You said you took a boat."

He smiles. "Yes, to leave *West* Germany. But I first had to flee *East* Germany. I did that by hiding in a refrigerated truck under the bodies of slaughtered pigs."

I stick out my tongue and scrunch up my face, wriggle

at the idea of pig blood dripping on me. "Ew! That's disgusting! You're kidding, aren't you?"

He laughs. "I thought you would enjoy that. It is a true story, but not mine. I hid under bags of grain. You must understand, in times of conflict and hostility, many did what they normally wouldn't do. The Berlin Zoo employees ate crocodile soup for weeks after the zoo was bombed in 1943. They had to do something with the dead animals."

Why would anyone bomb a zoo? I wonder what other foods they had to make. Elephant stew? Lion burgers? Orangutan sandwiches?

"Many Berliners fled from East to West. Werner assured me he and my mother would follow. The longer they took, however, the harder it became to leave. The government ordered a concrete wall, alarmed fencing, attack dogs, observation towers—even landmines—to keep the East Germans in the East. Many still tried. Many were killed for trying. Werner made the decision to send me his treasure—his valuable stamp collection—for safekeeping."

Stamps, little pieces of paper. That's what needed safekeeping? Millions of people were handed over to the Nazis, but the stamps stayed safe. Toots Meretsky didn't even need stamps. He hand-delivered his letters.

"Why were they so valuable?" I need some sort of reason,

some sort of justification for saving stamps, not people. But I already know any answer I get won't be good enough.

"They were worth a lot of money, but more than that, they were all Werner had left. Everything else was destroyed when our home was bombed, quite late in the war. Our home looked like Elvy's dollhouse. Walls and stairs still standing but the face completely torn off. We climbed those rickety stairs to rescue whatever we could. There wasn't much that hadn't been eaten up by fire. I found my metal box with my keepsakes; Werner found his metal box with his stamps. It was a dangerous thing to do, climb those stairs, go into a building that could crumble at any moment, but we wanted something, anything from our old lives."

It's an answer, but it's not good enough. "What was in your metal box?"

"Ah, nothing so financially significant, but important to me. You have seen a few of the items. *Naja*, Werner was worried the ruling Communists, who read and resealed whatever mail they so chose, would seize the collection if he simply put it in an envelope. So, he mailed each precious stamp under a regular stamp to avoid detection. When I received the letters, I was to soak the envelopes to remove and separate both layers."

"You never showed me them." I drop my feet to the floor and lean over the metal arm of Opa's bed. He's staring at the ceiling, at some far-off place only he can see. He cringes, his face and body tighten, from memories or from pain, I'm not sure which. Part of me wants to stroke his arm, the other doesn't want to touch him. I rest my hand on the metal bar. Stuck in the middle.

"*Nein*. Those, I haven't shown to anyone."

A nurse comes in to shift Opa around to prevent bedsores and give him a new bag of morphine to relieve his pain.

I check on the game between the Boateng brothers. Already into the second half with no goals from either team. Hold on, hold on, Müller's got the ball. He makes what looks like—for him—an easy cross to Mario Götze in front of the goalkeeper's box. With two guys on him, Götze butts it with his head. It bounces off his knee and—

"Yes!" I jump out of my chair, high-five my nonexistent teammates, and do a little dance. I cannot dance. Mr. Snorer watches me with his nose all crinkled up in disgust, Mr. Gargler with a giant yellowed-toothed smile.

"It's not a private room, kid. Sit down," Mr. Snorer yells, his slight Japanese accent coming out strong.

"Leave him be, Jimmu. He's happy. It's good to see some joy in the world. Go on, son, dance your heart out," says Mr. Gargler as he closes his eyes. His accent is like Opa's, but different.

Mr. Snorer grumbles and attempts to turn his television even louder, which I don't think is possible. Each clash of metal already shakes the entire hospital floor.

Ghana's got the ball now and, with almost the exact same set-up as between Müller and Götze, a Ghanaian heads it right in. So much for my celebration. Manuel Neuer's usually a chill guy, but he's looking pretty angry. I wish Weidenfeller was in net. He's on the national team, but as backup keeper. To Neuer. Who's on Bayern. Blech. Two goals, three minutes apart. Tie.

"I don't remember Uncle Werner." I sit back down and prop my feet on the corner of the bed.

"He never came to Canada. He was beaten and died not long after I left," Opa says quietly, his frail body shrinking into his bed. He swallows hard and starts coughing. I pour some water and hand him the glass. He reaches a shaky hand, and I know he won't be able to hold it on his own. I bring the glass to his lips, his hand holding mine. Protective. Comforting. My anger dies a bit as my dying grandfather's warmth fills me.

"He lived through the war only to be beaten to death?" I ask, more gently this time.

"Werner had few friends, but those friends knew about the stamp collection. When you're desperate, you do what you can to stay alive. They don't always make sense, your choices, but you make them because you have a family. They need to eat."

His friends beat him up for stamps? That's insane. They should have asked the zookeepers for some of their crocodile soup. Uncle Werner didn't even have the stupid—

"Oh my God, Opa, you had the stamps."

"Yes, I still do. I bet you can find them in your sleep." Opa closes his eyes but his uneasy breathing tells me he's still awake.

"So he was killed for no reason."

"Many people are killed for no reason. Sixty million people died during World War Two. How many of those people do you think had a reason to be killed? Did Calynn have a reason?"

Calynn's name sends a shiver through me. There's got to be a reason. *The motive surrounding the incident remains under investigation,* the newspaper article said. A teenage girl doesn't just break her neck on a rotten step, especially when she should never have been near the step to begin with.

"They're just stamps," I say quietly.

"Not to Werner. And not to me. They are all I have of my brother." Opa opens his eyes and goes back to staring at the TV. "You must take advantage of everything life gives you, Liam. You never know when life will be taken away. I want you and Elvy to experience the world, together. Spin a globe, put down a finger, and go. Meet others unlike yourselves, share a meal with them, listen to their stories—that's how we learn to get along."

Opa starts coughing and takes my hand with the glass. I bring it back to his lips.

"Danke, mein Prinz."

"Do you think the Boateng brothers get along?" I ask, keeping my hand with his.

Opa smiles, then burrows down into the pillows and closes his eyes again. "I hope the game ends in a tie."

"*Guten Tag, Vati,*" Dad says as he enters Opa's room, Elvy and Mom behind him. "How was the game?"

"Ended in a tie," I say.

He greets Mr. Gargler and Mr. Snorer—who turns down the volume on the TV.

"And how was your visit?" Dad asks, his hair and beard looking scragglier, his button-down shirt untucked from his jeans—not normal for him.

"I'm teaching him about soccer," Opa replies.

I roll my eyes and half-smile. Opa's "soccer" lessons all tie back to death and involve not actually watching soccer. The room is feeling cramped with seven of us in here now, so I say goodbye to Opa and head out to the waiting area. Maybe I can catch the recap there.

Two little girls in frilly pink dresses are watching some trippy cartoon with a tiger in a superhero mask, a white rabbit sidekick—which I'm pretty sure tigers eat—and some supervillain octopus trying to lure them into its underwater lair with a path of steaks. I sit down, rummage through my knapsack, and pull out the laminated newspaper articles.

Shocked family and friends are still reeling from the death of the teen who is remembered for her athleticism, warmth, intelligence, and humor. She and sister Azalea were dynamos on the soccer field, together leading the County Cougars to back-to-back championship titles. Both were already being lured with athletic scholarships to several universities and colleges across North America.

Calynn had a sister. Two soccer dynamos. Like the Boateng brothers. Geez. I think about what it must be like to have everything going for you—and then over, just like that. I wonder if that's what Coach thinks about me.

Everything going for me and I'm blowing it. What did Opa just say? *Take advantage of everything life gives you. You never know when life will be taken away.* Soccer is my life, and I definitely don't want it taken away, but it's not my *life*.

The rush of water from the trippy cartoon fills my ears, waves clapping against stone. The wind picks up and the cedars that shoot out of the cliff at weird angles violently shake scholarship papers and championship medals. Two little girls are in the water, sitting on a U-boat, throwing steaks at each other, and laughing. Can't they see Calynn, dead in a pink frilly dress? "Help her!" I scream. "Help me help her!" I stare at the body. Was repair-guy with you at Opa's the next time? The last time? Did he see you fall? Did he make you fall? Why is that rabbit hopping toward the U-boat with the supervillain covered in stamps?

"Liam." My mom is running her hand along my face. I open my eyes and focus. She's biting her bottom lip. She's wearing jeans and a T-shirt of a band I've never heard of, also untucked, the way she likes it, her curly brown hair held back in a loose ponytail, off her tanned face, her brown eyes watching me. Elvy looks a lot like her. I shift my gaze to the two little girls, eyes wide and mouths open. I'm guessing I screamed out loud. Again.

When we make eye contact, they squeak their chairs back and run out of the room.

"I take it those articles are from Alessia. Akin's gone crazy with that laminator." I quickly shove the articles back in my bag, feel a pain shoot along the back of my neck from the awkward way my head was resting on the chair, and rub it. Mom grabs the remote and switches to the sports channel with the soccer recap.

"You want to talk?" she asks. Of course she asks. "You haven't been sleeping. Are these chairs more comfortable?" Funny. She's always trying to find the funny. The little thing we can laugh at. Jewish humor. Sometimes it works. Sometimes it doesn't.

She turns a chair to face me, looks me straight in the eyes so I can't look away. "You are having a normal reaction to a not-normal situation, sweetheart." She pauses to make sure I'm listening. I don't have much choice, even if I desperately want to shift my eyes to the recap. "It's okay to feel anxious, to be frustrated and angry, and to question the screwy way the world works. It's not okay to keep it all bottled up. You'll explode. You have to be honest with yourself."

"People see dead bodies all the time," I say.

"If you're a coroner or work in the funeral business.

Otherwise, I would hope not so much. But you're also worrying about soccer, visiting your dying grandfather, and hearing stories about death and destruction. It's overwhelming. And it's not over yet."

She means Opa. He's not over yet. I pick up the remote and twirl it in my fingers. "The World Cup's going well."

She smiles. "Well, at least that's something." She dips out of view, comes back with two cups of water, and turns the chair to sit next to me. I take a look at the TV, but it's useless. Nothing registers.

"Mom, Opa's got a drawer full of little containers, jam, peanut butter, stuff like that. What's he saving them for?"

"That's what they did during the war, saved everything because they never knew when they'd need it." She props her feet up on the same chair as mine. I move my feet over a bit to make room. Considering Opa's hardly eating, I don't know what good those containers are.

"The war's been over for, like, a thousand years."

"Sixty-nine years. Some habits are hard to break," Mom says.

"Like Dad going to the County every weekend." I think about Dad and his insistence on going to Opa's house today, even though we'll have missed most of the day.

"You noticed that, did you?"

"You're going to have a hell of a time cleaning out Opa's house, aren't you?"

"Don't say hell, and yes. But that's for your dad and your aunt to do."

"I can help Dad."

"I bet he'd like that. He needs you."

We smile, clink cups like a toast, and both take a sip. Maybe I'll find the stamp collection.

CHAPTER 13

Saturday, June 21 – Prince Edward County

"Come on, sweethearts, time to wake up," Mom say. My eyes shoot open. Brightness strikes my eyeballs like a spaceship beam. I shield my eyes with my hand and focus. The porch light stabs its way through the pitch-black night, throwing shadowy light into the car. Elvy rolls her head from side to side, moaning like she was in a deep sleep. I'm sure she was sleeping, but I don't buy the whole I-can't-get-up-Daddy-carry-me act. When no one comes to sweep her into their arms, she grabs her bear stuffie, opens the car door, and zombie-walks into Opa's house. I shove my phone and laminated articles into my knapsack, throw it over a shoulder, and grab my soccer ball.

"Grab something else, too, buddy," Mom says, the

moment my feet leave the floor mat and hit the rocky ground.

"Elvy didn't."

"She's nine and should have been in bed hours ago."

I check out the trunk to pick my extra load carefully. Not too heavy, not too light, just right, so I don't have to come back out and help more. Bags of groceries, Elvy's suitcase, Mom and Dad's suitcase, storage boxes, bicycle helmets, washed linens, cooler. I grab a couple of grocery bags and head to the house.

The air buzzes with mosquitoes, even buzzier as I get closer to the porch light. I glance up to see the white bulb covered with them. I bet they're planning what to do about the nearby spiders and their webs of death. I bang on the wood door with my foot, making the lockbox hanging on the doorknob rattle. The lockbox was Opa's way of leaving the house key for whoever needed it when he'd go for long stays in Toronto. Pop in the code, pull out the key.

Dad opens the door just enough for me to slip in with everything I'm carrying. He thinks it'll reduce the number of mosquitoes that fly in with me. It doesn't. I'll have to remember to sleep with every body part under the blanket tonight.

"Oh God, what's that smell?" I ask, thinking someone left out sauerkraut—this German fermented cabbage thing that stinks like rotten eggs and gym socks, and that Opa eats by the bucketful. Ate, I guess. I doubt they serve it at the hospital and, even if they did, he can hardly down a sip of water, never mind chopped-up cabbage. Elvy and I want to puke every time Dad makes us eat it. "It's part of your heritage," he says. He doesn't say that when we ask for soft, salty German pretzels. He claims those aren't part of a healthy diet.

"The house just needs airing out. It's our first time up since—" Dad stops.

Since Calynn. We get it even if you don't say it, Dad.

The house always needs airing out. He goes to open the curtains, but they're already partly open. Dad's super-thorough in closing up the house, even if we did leave in a hurry the last time. He's got this mental checklist that he's been doing in the same order in the same way ever since he was a kid, when Opa's house was their family cottage and Opa still lived in Toronto, working as an architect. Dad would never leave the curtains in a way that people can see into the house.

I scan the living room. The orange-and-brown floral carpet is as old as Opa, and probably oozing toxic fumes. Our clothes always stink after being here, too. Dad says it's the smell of cedar, which is what Opa built the house out of. Mom says it's mold. Once a year she scrubs the walls from top to bottom. It doesn't help. She did manage to get rid of the hideous red and white curtains that hung in every room and over every window and that smelled like forty years of cooking—forty years of sauerkraut. But that was because she tried to wash them and they fell apart in the machine.

The fireplace mantel is packed with school photos of me and Elvy. Covering the entire far wall are framed black and white posters and prints that are totally brutal—a woman with hollow black circles for eyes, holding scared-looking kids, and the people behind her blindfolded, or maybe blind; another of a mother with what looks like a child's corpse in her lap. Opa says they have to do with war and injustice. Why you'd want to look at war on your walls when you lived through it in real life makes no sense to me.

On the shelf below the pictures, gazillions of books on everything from art to science to travel to the Wild West, and tons of decomposing English and German paperbacks written by Steinbeck, Emerson, Hesse, Remarque, and others Mom says I should read. I don't like reading in school; why would I read outside of school? There are handrails around the room and stair rails that were installed only a few months ago for the all-of-three steps to the kitchen. Dad insisted they be put in if Opa was going to keep living on his own. He worried he'd slip and fall and hurt himself. He never imagined cancer would hurt him first.

I bring the groceries into the kitchen. The gross smell gets grosser. I can't see any sauerkraut—or other food, for that matter—on the stone counters or the kitchen table, just a police business card. I open the fridge. Mom calls the color avocado and the style vintage. I call the color puke-green and the style "has to be repaired every other month." No smell inside. I look in the matching toaster, burnt toast smell, and the matching oven, baked-on-black-stuff smell. I open the pantry.

"Aahhhh!" I jump back and slam the door.

"What's the matter?" Elvy says from behind me, freaking me out all over again. I thought she went to bed. Little faker.

"Don't!" I yell, but she opens the pantry door anyway. A thin lifeless tail hangs down.

"Aww, poor mousy." She grabs a plastic bag from under the sink, climbs on a chair to get a better look at the curled-up mouse carcass by the jar of peanut butter, then picks it up with the bag and seals it.

"Here you go, Daddy." She drops the mouse bag in front of his feet. Gross.

I should have let her go find the fossils by herself. Maybe she would have bagged the dead girl before I saw her. See her. Still see her. Elvy stares at her stuffed animals on the living room sofa. "Who played with my stuffies?"

Like Dad, she's very particular about things being left exactly the right way.

"Maybe the mouse did," I answer.

"Ha, ha." She glances at the curtains, now fully opened, looks back at her stuffed animals, then looks at me, her eyes wide. I bite my bottom lip. She scrunches her face, like she's thinking real hard. I wonder if she's come to the same conclusion as me: someone—besides a mouse—has been in the house. She rearranges the stuffed animals the way she needs them to be, then heads back to our bedroom.

I grab my soccer ball and head outside, to the end of the porch that juts out over the cliff's edge. It's so dark out, I can't even see the lake. Tree frogs croak to one another in different deep sounds. The smell of lavender from Opa's garden comes and goes with the wind. At the bottom of the cliff, the water slaps the shore, the shore where I found Calynn. My heart beats faster the more I think about her. I lie down on the sun-bleached porch boards, same color as the dead mouse, and rest the soccer ball on my stomach. I stare up at the black sky with its explosion of stars. Here one day. Gone the next.

I try to find something other than the Big Dipper. Opa used to set up his telescope right here where I'm lying, then he'd open one of his thousands of books to show me a picture of a constellation, and we'd search the sky for it.

Did you see the constellations after you fell, Calynn? Did you see turkey vultures circling? Did you see the face of the person who killed you?

Whoa. I just turned the accident, possibly foul play, into murder. My chest pounds like the soldiers' boots on the sandy beach.

I hear the footsteps, then see the long shadow. Dad. He lies down next to me and extends his arms to hold his tablet to the sky. It reads the stars, then links them, like a connect-the-dots, to form shapes. Names of the constellations show up: Canes Venatici, which looks like two dogs; Bootes, which is some guy; Draco, a dragon. He moves the screen and it starts again. Ursa Major, Lynx, Camelopardalis, which isn't a camel at all. It's a giraffe.

"That's cool," I say. It's the first time Dad and I have spent any time together in I don't know how long. No, I do. Since Opa got really sick.

"Thought I'd try looking at things your way." He closes the tablet. "You want to talk?"

"I love it here," I blurt out. The nasty carpet, the lifting linoleum, the moldy smell, the falling-apart books, the puke-green appliances, the dead mouse, the croaking frogs, the mosquitoes feasting on my legs and arms. The endless stars. Opa. "Can we move here?"

Dad pats my arm. "We can keep coming." He doesn't say *after Opa dies*, which is what he means. Parents think if they don't say things, then we don't know things. It's like when he and Opa speak German. Like it's some secret code. They don't realize they've been speaking it since I was born and I learned the language. And I understand very well.

Dad swats at his legs, then goes back in the house. I stay a few more minutes. When I feel like every pore of my skin is another mosquito bite, I surrender and go inside. I spray myself with the anti-itching stuff Mom left out, then climb the rope ladder to the top bunk in the room I share with Elvy, and cover myself with the striped Hudson's Bay blanket.

I stare at my soccer posters on the ceiling. Weidenfeller. Lewandowski. Dortmund. Germany. Weidenfeller. Lewandowski. Dortmund. Germany. I'm wide awake.

And itchy. I scale down the rope ladder and check on Elvy. She's snuggled up in her pink and purple owl blanket. That blanket creeps me out. The stupid owl eyes glow at night. I move in closer. The night light casts an orange-yellow light on Elvy's face, just enough to see that her eyes are definitely closed. She purrs when she sleeps. I wonder how I can use that against her. I consider waking her up, to come to the garage with me to investigate, but decide I should just let her sleep.

I tiptoe out of the room alone. The house is stuffy and smells like vinegar from Mom sterilizing the kitchen, but at least the dead mouse smell is gone. I grab the garage key hanging by the front door, stop at Opa's desk. Two piles of opened envelopes, one with a yellow sticky note that says paid, one with a pink sticky note that says *to be paid*. I flip through both piles, find an envelope marked *Geyer and Son Repairs*. The stamp wasn't postmarked, which means it was delivered instead. I pull out the letter, an invoice for the railing work, and look at the date. Opa's birthday. I put it back in the envelope and on the desk.

I quietly open the back door and walk out onto the back porch. The cedars are so overgrown there isn't a sliver of moonlight to guide me. Gnarled trunks and fallen branches from summer and winter storms look like giant tree people. Limbs in offence position, the wind whispering the plan of attack.

I unlock the garage and lift the metal door. It creaks, but I only move it high enough to slip in.

"Ow, what the hell!" I look down. I tripped over my bicycle that I still didn't put away. Opa bought this bike to get to all those different jobs in *West* Germany after the whole escape from the East—details he didn't mention in his letter—so he could buy a boat ticket for Canada. The wheel rims are rusted, the white leather seat is cracked, and the red paint is peeling. It should have been tossed a long time ago, but I like riding it. I leave it on the ground, but make a mental note to watch for it on my way out. I pull a cord hanging from all the way up to the rafters, and a dim light flickers to life. The rest of the bikes lean against a pile of wood for projects Opa never got around to—a treehouse, a new dock, a new set of stairs to the lake.

Why did Opa need George to come into the garage? Why did Calynn come instead? Did her grandfather ask her to? Opa's stories keep distracting me from remembering to ask about the garage, which is so crammed with stuff you really have to know what you're looking for to find it. I scan; try to focus. Not my specialty. Kayak. Canoe. Paddles. Windsurfer. Rusting filing cabinet. Archery stuff.

Rusted wood stove. Coiled rope. Metal strongboxes. One, two, three, four. *Fotos. Dokumente. Kinder. Bärchen.* Photos, documents, children, little bear—Opa's nickname for my grandmother. I do remember coming to the garage every now and then with Opa, just the two of us, and him showing me some of his prized possessions in these boxes. I just don't remember what they are.

One box is missing, though. Which one? Think, think.

I make my way to the back shelves, climbing over sawhorses, lawnmowers, wood flooring, moldy furniture. I understand why Opa saves everything, but I can't understand what he'd need most of this stuff for. What are you going to do with a blowfish skeleton hanging from the rafters?

"Ow!" My back hits the side of the windsurfer and I take the board down with me as I tumble to the dirt ground, my foot caught in an ancient patio chair's plastic strips. I am not having a good night. I lift myself up, brush forty years of dirt and who knows what off myself, and pull the plastic away to untangle my foot.

If Calynn broke through a step like I just broke through the chair, then she would have fallen, maybe twisted an ankle or something, but I doubt she would have broken her neck. And she would have landed close to the step, not close to the water, like I drew on my map of not-New France, like I see seared in my brain. She must have been running down the stairs. Why would she leave the garage, if she even came in here, and run down the danger-taped stairs to the lake? Unless she was being chased ... but by who? And why?

I look around for the missing box. God, there's a lot of crap in here. And dust. And ...

"Aahhhh!" Something slithers across my foot. I jump real quick and it moves to the filing cabinet. Ew. I am not meant for country life. I tiptoe to keep any other snakes or mice living in here asleep, and find the missing box propped on the radial saw next to my Zaidie's homemade baseball bat. It doesn't hit very well, but it's cool to look at.

Like the other boxes, this one's dark reddish-black, kinda like Elvy's hair, and about the size of a shoebox, but the shape is a little different from the others, and the hinged top is all dented, like Ryder's locker. I look at the label on the box: *Deutschland*. Germany. I bet this is the actual box he rescued from his bombed home.

I grab a pair of gardening gloves like I've seen on *Sherlock* or some other TV detective show, so I don't tamper with evidence. I open the lid, down but not properly closed or locked. Not much is inside: A tiny wind-up music box, some old German money, a cigarette carton filled with little flags from different countries, a ticket for the 1936 Olympics. One side of the ticket has a thick pink-patterned stripe, broken up with the words for section and seat and stuff I can't translate. The main part is beige, with a grayish illustration of the Olympiastadion and red wording: "XI. OLYMPIADE BERLIN 1936," "*Eröffnungsfeier*," "1, AUG. 16.00 *UHR*" and more.

I'm sure Opa's shown me this stuff before, but I never really thought much about it and forgot about it. Now that I know the story behind the ticket, it's pretty cool. I wonder if Opa's going to tell me stories about these other things, too. I'm pretty sure the strongbox had more stuff in it. Think, think.

I close the box, put it back in its place on the shelf, and grab the baseball bat as I quietly slip out of the garage, stepping over my bike, and back into my room. Elvy's still asleep. I put the bat on top of the bookshelf, then lie down and stare at my soccer posters.

Curtains open. Stuffed animals out of place. Strongbox unlocked, something missing.

Letters. Letters from Germany are missing.

Is that what Opa wanted, a pack of letters? Calynn didn't have them with her on the shore. Unless they washed away? They couldn't have all washed away, unless they were all together in an envelope or an elastic band or something, which I don't remember them being. Not in the box, anyway. Someone came with Calynn. Drove her, left her, took the letters.

But someone's also been here since.

CHAPTER 14

Wednesday, June 25 – Toronto

We're up four to two, second half, five minutes left on the clock. A lot can happen between now and that whistle. I'm back in net and I have to stay focused. Be on the ball, like Coach says. We're playing the Hornets tonight, and they're the best in the league. They aren't going to let us win four-two. It's not in their DNA. Their DNA is actually made up of vengeance, brutality, and height. Every single one of their players towers over us. It's like they were recruited from some basketball team.

Only they're good. Real good. Like the mid coming down the line right now. He's got awesome footwork, and he and his wing are passing back and forth and, as they do, they're picking off our guys. Ryder's on defense. He rams right for their forward in a kind of take-no-prisoners way you see in superhero movies.

The forward blocks and passes back to the wing. Kai is on that guy and they do this dance—Kai trying to keep the guy from kicking, the guy trying to keep Kai from taking the ball. Kai manages a tap, sending the ball off the field, enough for a throw-in. Their wing grabs the ball on the sideline, looks around the field. He sees the forward, gives the tiniest nod, and throws the ball toward his mid. Weird. Xavion intercepts, but another Hornet steals and boots the ball up over everyone, landing right before their forward, who charges toward me. I'm trying to read him while watching the ball, but he's not changing his pace, he's not positioning himself to shoot, he's not—

Oof!

I'm blasted by his body and fall backwards. When I sit up, I see the forward running the field with his arms up. He scored? That can't be legal! Ryder pulls me up, and I head to the ref to complain and get the guy carded. He shakes his head and tells me to get back in net.

Both teams get into position for the remaining minutes. My stomach hurts where the forward barreled his fist into me, but I don't let it show. We're still up four to three.

The final whistle blows. We win. My team doesn't line

up to shake hands with the Hornets, but Coach yells at us and, since goalkeepers are first to shake, I lead our team to do the right thing. Players from both teams aggressively knock each other with their shoulders as we file past. The forward smiles at me like he wants to beat the crap out of me. He already did, and I'm still standing. So much for the beautiful game.

"I can't believe he didn't get carded," I mumble to Ryder as we walk off the field.

"He didn't get carded because you were in the Twilight Zone again," Coach says, without any hint of humor.

"What? He attacked me." I stand solid in front of her.

"I don't think so." She gives me a laser-eye stare.

I want to melt, but I won't. I didn't do anything wrong. Ryder, Xavion, Kai, and Arjun move away from me and Coach, but not so far they can't overhear. They start packing up their bags. Very. Slowly.

"I know so. And everyone else on our team knows so," I say, staring right back at her. "I can't believe you're blaming me for his illegal move."

"I'm blaming you for not focusing on what's going on right in front of your eyes."

"I can tell you every single thing that happened in this game. I can't explain it, because it seems to me everyone's gone crazy and forgotten the rules. I can tell you those, too." I walk to my bag, pull on my Dortmund hoodie, and grab my Dortmund hat.

"Liam." Coach jogs up to me and grabs my arm before I can put my hat on my head. "We need to talk."

I look at her mammoth hand on my ropey arm, made slightly bigger by the padding in my keeper jersey. Out of the corner of my eye, I see Ryder, Xavion, Kai, and Arjun quietly shuffling closer, but not too close. I look Coach straight in the eyes. I feel nothing.

"I've canceled the tryout," she says softly. She sounds like the therapist, all syrupy sweet and caring. "Five weeks isn't enough time to get your head back to where it needs to be. If I put you in there and you fail ... Liam, you won't get an opportunity like this again."

"Yeah, I won't. Because if I don't get in now at the start of the program, they'll never take me."

I look at her hand, still on my arm. I put my Dortmund hat on my head in some sort of act of defiance, maybe. I don't know. She doesn't react. She just stares at me, like she's waiting for me to understand. That she's ruining my life, yeah, I understand.

"You get one shot to make a first impression. I know you can make it. I want you to make it. I want you to go pro like you've been dreaming, but you have a thousand other things on your mind. The guys over there, they don't care. Not until you're on their team. We'll figure something else out."

I glance at Ryder, Xavion, Kai, and Arjun sitting on the grass, elbows on knees, mouths gaping, silent, not moving, like they've been petrified by a basilisk.

"Liam, are you listening to me?" Coach gives me a little shake, then smiles like everything's okay now that she's had her say, like she's got my best interests at heart. Maybe she does, but I'm not buying it.

"Yeah, I'm listening to you. Are you listening to me?" I yank my arm from her grip and look her straight in the eyes. "I quit."

Mom and I, and even Elvy, don't talk the whole way to the car. We don't talk the whole way home. I stare out the window and watch the field fade away. Along with my soccer career.

CHAPTER 15

Thursday, June 26 – Toronto

No one ever in the history of last days of school wants to be in school on the last day. Class 7B seems to be the exception. When I get to Ms. Guerrero's room, everyone's already there. Okay, that's not the surprising part. I'm usually last. It's the way they all look at me when I walk into the room. Like they were caught in the act—of what, I have no idea.

"So, we've been thinking," says Reagan, following me as I head to my desk.

"And talking," says Ryder, turning around in his desk to face me.

"And writing," says Kane, sitting next to me already, but moving his face really close to mine in that way that creeps me out.

Okaaaay.

It's like they wrote out a little play again, making sure everyone gets a turn and the same amount of lines, although this time, I'm not sure what the subject is. So far as I can tell, it's sci-fi horror. They're all acting weirder than usual, like maybe their bodies have been taken over by aliens, and I'm feeling pretty freaked out and uncomfortable, kinda like I imagine those people must have felt escaping under dead pigs. Okay, maybe not *that* freaked out and uncomfortable.

"We put together a package for your grandfather," Reagan starts again.

"Let me get this straight. You all came to the *last day* of school early to work on a package for my grandfather?" I say this more like a statement than a question.

"A gift really, but yeah," says Ryder, passing me a white-and-blue file folder box. I take off the top and look inside.

"I baked him oatmeal-raisin cookies," Reagan says, pulling out an old-looking metal container with paintings of Berlin landmarks on the top and sides. The Brandenburg Gate is the only thing I recognize, but the words Berlin are scrawled on the front, so .... Reagan sees me staring at it. "No biggie, my mom ordered it online."

Along with the cookies, the box is filled with drawings—

the Brandenburg Gate again, some weird tower with a ball in the middle, a huge government-looking building with a dome on top, soccer stadiums, and even one of the buildings in Toronto Opa designed, according to the message written on the bottom. How did they know he designed it? Someone obviously paid close attention during Opa's architecture talk. There's a plush soccer ball and photos from this year—our class photo, along with a bunch of others with me and my friends. And a stack of World Cup sheets marked up with everyone's bets for who's going to win.

Alessia slides a letter across my desk. "This explains everything."

I look up at Ms. Guerrero, who isn't wearing her glasses today.

But she's wearing a huge smile. She juts out her chin, motioning for me to read the letter, all perfectly typed up and signed again, but this time with small flags next to each name—China, Italy, Jamaica, France, and others I do and don't recognize. Like they're telling Opa their families came to Canada from somewhere else, too. Weird. And pretty cool.

Dear Mr. Reimold,

Thank you so much for your letter answering our questions

about World War Two. We learned a lot, which made our social studies teacher, Ms. Guerrero, very happy.

Most of us have heard you speak when you came to school to talk about architecture, or met you at soccer games. Your letter made us feel like we know you even more. We know there isn't much we can say to comfort you at this time, but we thought we'd send along some things that Liam can put around your room that might make you smile.

Good luck with the World Cup! Go Germany go!

Class 7B

"Hi Opa," I say as I drop the file folder box on the table with the TV and grab the remote to find the game. Flick, flick, flick. I sit in my chair and prop my feet up on the bed. I avoid looking at Opa. I don't want him to see my eyes, which are still red from that letter and the gifts. I never realized Opa made such an impression on them.

"*Mein Prinz*, how was soccer last night? Give me the play by play."

I can't believe he remembered. How does he even know what day it is? Every single day in here is the same.

"It was fine. Not much to talk about," I say quickly to get it out of the way. No point in telling Opa that I quit, that it's over. I don't care, anyway. Really. The games, the playing, they haven't been as much fun without Opa training me, without him showing up the past few months, without him calling to find out how they went. Maybe ... maybe I was just playing for him. To be with him. "Can I ask you a question?" The sportscasters are talking highlights and heavy rain and showing past footage in the pre-game.

"*Ja, natürlich.*" He slowly moves an arm over the side of the bed to find the switch that makes his head and back raise up. I stand to help him, but he rolls his head from side to side. I sit back down.

"Was Calynn getting letters from the garage?" I ask.

"Letters? *Nein.*" The bed buzzes as it moves.

"If you tell me what she was getting, I can get it."

"*Danke,* but your father has already looked. George asked me if he could do anything. It seemed such an innocent request. I do not understand why Calynn went or what happened, but I hope we find out."

So much for Opa accepting and moving on, like Coach said. His eyes are also red, wet. I wonder if he was thinking about Calynn's death before I got here. Or his own.

I think about what Opa said in the letter to school: *Only by thinking about the past can we have a future.*

And what Coach said: *You keep thinking about the past, you're not going to have a future*. Who's right?

"Who's playing today?" Opa's staring at the TV, where flags for the U.S. and Germany are taking up half the screen. Opa has worn glasses for as long as I can remember, but he's never had a problem seeing the TV before. I stand back up and push the TV to the end of the dresser closest to Opa. Then decide to push the whole dresser closer.

"*Ah, danke, mein Prinz*. I see now."

I can't believe they even have to play this game. I mean, really? Germany is going to obliterate the States. Which is good, because I don't know how well I can watch today. Everything looks a bit blurry. Out of the corner of my eye, I catch Mr. Snorer holding out the remote toward his TV and shaking it. He's trying to turn the volume up, up, up, but nothing happens. I go over and hold out my hand for the remote. I glance at the screen—everything is black and white, and the actors make a lot of exaggerated movements. Blech, it's a silent movie. At the volume he's hit, the commercials will sound like we're under attack. I turn back to Opa and notice Mr. Gargler, in the bed next to his, watching me, a sad smile on his normally happy face. No one's doing well in here today. Mr. Gargler sees me see him, and his sad smile changes to a toothy grin. He waves hello and I wave back.

"I saw the U.S. versus Germany once before. I was sixteen years old. A kid." Opa's speech is slow, slower than usual, but once he gets going, the more normal he tends to sound. I move back to my chair and look at the countdown clock on the screen. Ten minutes until kick-off. Here we go.

"That's when I had to leave home. For the army. Sixteen. It was nearing the end of the war and Germany was losing, but Hitler wasn't prepared to lose. So he got everyone who could walk and talk, forced a gun in their hands, and told them they were now soldiers. I had three days of training, then I was sent to the front."

A real buff guy, who's got to be seven feet tall, comes into the room, carrying a tray of food—lunch, I guess. He rolls the wheelie table up to Mr. Gargler's chest, then takes off the tray cover. He does the same for Mr. Snorer and then for Opa. Not one of them lifts a hand to eat.

"We were two young guys and two old men, thrown together in a foxhole on a ridge in the woods. Others in our militia were in their own foxholes on either side of a road. None of us had a clue what to do, but we knew we were supposed to stop the American army. Their soldiers and tanks were along the road, shooting at buildings, firing on the village. They obliterated it. I can't remember the name of the village anymore. I don't know if it ever recovered." Opa's voice cracks.

I imagine my neighborhood disappearing in an instant. Just. Like. That. All my stuff up in flames. Even then, when the fire is out, going back, but having nowhere and nothing to go back to. Do I have a prized possession like Opa did? Like Uncle Werner did? What would I risk my life to keep safe?

"We hid, hoping they wouldn't find us. I don't know if any of the four of us fired a shot. We had forty-eight rounds of ammunition and one *Panzerfaust*, an anti-tank weapon. We refused to use it. You had to be within one hundred meters of the target, the length of a soccer field—a suicide mission. We wanted to get out of there. Alive. The two older guys said to us, 'Don't you move.' They had wives, children back home. They protected us, as though we were their children. But they couldn't stop the firing. They couldn't stop the bombs from exploding, the grenades from launching, the tanks from rolling. And they sure as hell couldn't stop Hitler. Until he was gone, we were all as good as dead."

Opa's voice isn't choppy anymore. But it's quiet, full of fear and anger, like he's there. He stares at the ceiling, at some distant place, a place with bombs and grenades and tanks, I'm betting. I shiver and stare at the TV. No Hitler in the stands as the players come out.

"And then, just like that. Pow!" I jump at Opa's cry and booming handclap, like a pair of cymbals that wakes you from a good night's sleep in the concert hall your parents dragged you to. Speaking from experience.

"Günter, the other young man, dead. Right there. Before my eyes. His blood. Speckled all over my ill-fitting uniform, my boots. My face. I didn't hear the shot. But I heard the scream. I still hear the scream."

The starting whistle blows. So does my mind.

"One of the older men, he covered my mouth. I must have been screaming, too. He spoke to me, calmed me, told me he was going to get me out of there. Alive. As the Americans advanced, he pointed to a small dirt road behind the American line. I went out from the side of the ridge. Only me; they would not come. A man happened by with a cart of rags. I dug through, found some clothes, put them on, hid my weapon in the cart, and walked with the ragman like I was his child. We came to a little town. I wish I knew the name of it. That town was also filled with American soldiers but, somehow, I wasn't spotted. I hitchhiked on a German truck, which took me close to Berlin, and from there I made it home.

"Mother was glad to see me." He breathes in deep, wheezing. Like he didn't take a breath during that whole story. I don't actually think he did. I bring water to his lips, but he shakes his head. I put down the water and stroke his arm.

"So you abandoned your post," I say.

"Yes. I sure as hell did not want to fight, and I sure as hell did not want to die for something, someone I did not believe in." I've never heard Opa angry before. Even though he doesn't have the strength to speak loud and clear, I can hear the anger. Loud and clear.

"Mom and Dad don't like it when we say hell."

Opa makes a sound that's probably supposed to be a laugh, then takes my hand in his.

"The Americans are funny. One minute they are bombing Berlin, the next they are feeding it. Well, West Berlin, where your Oma lived."

That does seem strange. I bite. "How come?"

"The western half of Berlin was under American, British, and French rule after the war."

That makes sense. I guess. Not really. And it's kind of a boring answer, especially for Opa.

He turns his head to me and smiles. "You would like to know more?" He says this more like a statement than a question. I shrug. I kinda do. "Do you like candy?"

This just took a weird turn, but I nod anyway.

"The Soviets wanted West Berlin for themselves, so they blocked access to the city—or so they thought. The Allies took to the air and flew in food and supplies. At one point, a plane was landing every forty-five seconds. One plane, *der Rosinenbomber*, what the Americans call the candy bomber, dropped little parachutes of candy for the children. Oh, how that made your Oma happy."

Oma did love candy. She always had some on her and slipped Elvy and me a piece when she thought Mom and Dad weren't looking. Opa melts into his bed. He looks so thin. I wish I could get him to eat something. Anything. Even candy. I search through the file-folder box for Reagan's oatmeal-raisin cookies and offer him one. He shakes his head. I offer one to Mr. Snorer and Mr. Gargler. They also shake their heads. They still haven't touched their lunch. I prop my feet up on the bed, pull out a cookie, and take a bite. No bad, but I would have preferred chocolate chip.

"U.S. versus Germany. This will be a good game," Opa says.

CHAPTER 16

Friday, June 27 – Prince Edward County

Summer vacation. No one telling me to read. No one telling me to study. No one telling me to focus. No one telling me to—

"Liam, I told you to put the groceries away. Come on, I'm on vacation, too," Mom says, lugging out a new vacuum cleaner, a bucket of cleaning products, and a mop. I think she's planning a full-out war on the mold. Or the mice. Because she's definitely not cleaning the house as a welcome back for Opa.

I grab the grocery bags from the back of the car and drop them on the kitchen table, the police business card still there. I unpack a couple of boxes of Kraft Dinner and open the pantry door.

"Aahhhh!" I jump back. So red. So very, very red.

"Is that blood?" Elvy asks, standing by my side. "Look at those teeny tiny footprints."

Mom squats down next to Elvy.

"What the—" That comes from the basement. Elvy, Mom, and I run to Dad, who's standing in the cinder-block electrical room rubbing the top of his head real hard. Elvy being Elvy, she chops her way through the spider webs and pushes past him.

"Huh," she says. Great explanation.

Mom and I move in. There's a box of rat poison on the floor that's been nibbled and a very red, dehydrated something in the mousetrap just a foot away.

"We don't even use poison," Dad says. "I don't know where that box came from."

"Okay, kids, let's get out of here and let your father take care of it."

"Gee, thanks."

We go back to the kitchen and look at the pantry again. The dead red thing in the basement is the same color as the footprints on the shelf.

"It's red food dye," Mom says, pulling out a chewed-through dropper bottle from the back corner. "The darn mouse gnawed through the plastic."

"And then it went downstairs and found the poison," Elvy adds, looking around for more "teeny tiny" footprints, like she's Sherlock. He wouldn't waste his time on a case like this.

"Ate it up, and then it was so dehydrated, stepped into the trap," Mom finishes off.

"You're telling me the mouse made the cupboard look like a murder scene, then attempted suicide by eating poison, only to be killed in a trap?" I say. They both shrug. "That's insane!"

"Actually, I think it was high on caffeine, too." Mom waves some busted coffee pods in the air and then drops them into the trash. Ew. "Go outside, guys. I have a lot of sterilizing to do."

Elvy and I don't argue.

"You wanna go next door and catch tadpoles in the pond?" Elvy asks as I walk slowly, kicking stones along the path to nowhere.

"Nah." We veer toward the garage, Mom and Dad's cars parked in a clearing that once had an outhouse. Gross. She lifts the metal door with such a horror-movie creak, it gives me the freezes inside.

"You wanna go for a bike ride?" She picks up my bike and leans it against the others.

I shake my head.

"Bow and arrow?" She shimmies past the swing we've been meaning to hang on the old oak tree for the past three summers.

"Grass is too long. We'll never find the arrows, and then Dad will get mad when he mows," I say.

"We could mow."

I stare at Elvy. She stares at me. She swallows a giggle and chomps down on the lifting corners of her mouth, then bursts out laughing anyway. I crack up, too. Mowing! Good one. When we finally stop, we go back to scanning the garage for something, anything, to do.

My eyes stop at Opa's strongboxes and I make my way over to them. I pull down the Germany box and open it. Still not locked. Still no letters. I look at the Olympic ticket stub and think about everything it means: an event Hitler used to make Nazi Germany look good; Toots Meretsky and other Jewish athletes from around the world not backing down; a moment Opa shared with his father; a little piece of paper that survived the war. I put the ticket in my pocket, feel like Opa's here with me.

If Opa didn't ask for the letters, someone else took them. But for what?

And then it hits me. Little pieces of paper that survived the war.

The stamps.

Someone took the letters for Uncle Werner's stamps! The valuable collection that was worth a lot of money.

I race out of the garage and back to the house.

"Liam!" Elvy yells.

I don't answer. I can't answer. Not right now. I yank open the screen door and grab my knapsack.

"Liam, I said outside," Mom says.

I don't answer. I can't answer. Not right now. I shuffle through to find Alessia's first laminated newspaper. I pull it out, drop the bag, scan the backside of the news page. The side with all the annual events listed. Fishing ... tomatoes ... the annual Geyer coin and stamp show and sale. July fifth and sixth. Next weekend.

I shuffle through my knapsack again, pull out my phone, run into the kitchen, and spin the police business card around to read the number. My hands shake as I dial. My voice cracks as I speak.

"Hello, is this the police?"

When I find Elvy again, she's in the field, building a castle in the sand pile, a football by her feet. A new sport. I guess I should try a new sport. The long brushy grass grazes my shins, my legs still wobbly from the call, from discovering a motive. A reason. There has to be a reason. I hope I'm right. I hope it helps Calynn. I hope it helps Opa. I hope it helps me.

No, I'm fine.

Elvy grabs the ball and tosses it my way. It lands real short with hardly a thump and we both run for it. She picks it up and tries again. This time she goes long, and I have to run the other way to catch it. I jump like I think I should, but I miss as it arcs down just beyond my reach. Great, I can't catch a high football, either.

Thwack! It lands on a rock and rebounds toward my face. This time I catch it before it can do any damage.

"You ready?" I ask.

Elvy nods. I toss, she catches. She tosses, I catch. It's actually fun. Elvy bends over and starts counting in a real gruff voice.

"A hundred and two. Forty-eight. Seventy-five. Hike!" She giggles, then tosses the ball. I run and throw it down like I just scored a touchdown. When I go to pick it up, the creepiest insects I've ever seen are streaming out of the football's laces: skinny reddish-brown body, wings, antennae, pincers. Soon Elvy is next to me looking at what I'm not touching.

"That is so gross," Elvy says.

"It really is." We both keep watching.

"How many do you think that's been?" she asks, crouching down.

"I don't know. Ten?" They look like tiny soldiers on the march.

"How many do you think there are?" she asks, leaning closer to the ball.

"I'm not sure I want to know," I say, wondering how they got in there in the first place.

"Yeah, me neither." We keep watching. At least another ten come out. Country living is great, but disgusting at the same time.

A low hum, like endless thunder, takes our eyes off the ball and toward the sky, but there's nothing to see. We leave the football in the field and run back to the house, to the porch jutting out over Lake Ontario.

The hum is loud and getting louder. The military plane it's coming from is big and getting bigger. And bigger. God, it's huge. It's so low in the sky and so close to the cliff I can make out a dark gray maple leaf under its massive wing. As it passes overhead, the roar forces Elvy and me to cover our ears.

Through my hands I can make out the sound of gunfire. A hatch at the bottom of the plane opens and something starts falling. It's all slow motion at first against the black sky with its explosion of stars and constellations that I can't name, but then it plummets faster and faster.

KABOOM!

A huge explosion sets the village below on fire. Tanks roll along the road, mowing down whatever's in their way. Opa is holding an anti-tank weapon and he's within one foot of the target.

"It's a suicide mission!" I yell, but Opa smiles his big old Opa smile. And then, just like that. Blood. Speckled all over my ill-fitting uniform, my boots, my face.

"No!" I scream and run from the ridge, right into an oncoming soldier.

"Watch it, Liam!" My dad's holding a mug away from his body. "Where are you going so fast?"

"Liam's going on a suicide mission," Elvy says.

"I see." Dad hands me his mug and I sip. Chocolate milk. Weird.

I look back at the lake. The military plane is no bigger than Dad's old toy planes in our bedroom as it veers around the cliff. There was no gunfire. No bomb. No explosion. No village on fire. No anti-tank weapon. No suicide mission. No Opa. I drop onto a bench by the picnic table.

Dad follows my line of sight. "It's just a practice run. The Trenton air force base isn't too far."

"A practice run for ... war?" That doesn't sound good. That doesn't sound good at all.

"You're safe." Dad sits on the bench and puts an arm around me.

I don't feel safe. Military plane. Open curtains. Unlocked strongbox. Calynn's body. Opa's stories. Does Dad even know what Opa's been telling me? Did Opa tell him, ask him first? I clench my hands, my nails cutting into my palms.

Dad squeezes me tighter as Elvy snuggles up on his other side. "Life's full of good things and bad things, Liam. It's up to us to make sure the good outweighs the bad."

He knows. He definitely knows. And he's heard it all, too.

The hum is back. I tip my head and watch the military plane make its return trip.

I hope the hatch drops candy this time.

CHAPTER 17

Saturday, June 28 – Prince Edward County

"You can't do that!" I yell through the living room window of Opa's house. The one my mom is standing at with her hand to one ear, scrunching up one side of her face like she can't hear me. She locked the door. Actually locked Elvy and me out of the house—because it's a beautiful day, she said. I'm pretty sure that's illegal, like touching a soccer ball with your hands or butting an opponent in the head during a game. Like recruiting kids to be soldiers. The twenty bucks she gave us to go get ice cream before bolting the door doesn't get her off the hook. That's bribery. Or blackmail. One of those. Also illegal.

I head for the garage. Dad's car is gone. Back to the city to see Opa. I hop on Opa's red bicycle and meet up with Alessia and Elvy, who are waiting on the road by the No Trespassing sign. It's sweltering hot, but the ice cream factory is only a fifteen-minute ride away. The road looks wet, but every time we reach where that puddle should be it disappears. No one is ever on this road, except a chicken every now and then, but today there's a pack of power-cyclists spinning right past. We speed up a bit, can't catch the cyclists, go back to our slower pace. Birds tweet above the dried-up lilac bushes that line the road. A black sheepdog yaps louder and louder as we come to our first and only turn, at the dilapidated barn with very little of its red roof left. I can already smell chocolate in the air—which is pretty amazing since it has to compete with the smell of the cows from the factory's farm. At the halfway mark, we pass a rusted-out tractor that's been sitting in that same patch under the cedars and oaks for as long as I can remember. Once useful, now set out on the sidelines to die alone.

We race to the finish line, drop our bikes on the grass, and run into the Milky Way Bay store. Terrible name, amazing ice cream. A lineup of parents and grandparents fan themselves and check out other local products for sale—cheese, honey, mustard, lemonade—as little kids press their faces against the freezer, looking at their colorful choices. We get our cones—Fudge Brownie for me, Cotton Candy for Elvy, Cookie Dough for Alessia—and go back outside. Or try to. Elvy stops before the bright pink screen door. I bump into her but manage to save my cone from a terrible fate.

"What's the matter with you?" I ask.

She points. A small yellow car. Like the one Elvy insists she saw Calynn in.

"There's probably more than one 'teeny-tiny' yellow car in the County," I say. I push the screen door open, the tiny cowbell ringing out our exit, and walk around the car. A car like any other. Elvy and Alessia trail behind.

"It's the same car," Elvy whispers, stopping at the back bumper. A red County Cougars sticker is slapped on to the left side of the license plate.

"Oh," Alessia and I say at the same time. All three of us sit down on the bright pink wood bench facing the car and lick our ice cream.

The bell rings again, and out comes a guy who's so jacked, he looks like he's on a high school football team. He also looks like the repair guy in Alessia's photo. He's dressed in a blue work shirt and work pants, with the words *Geyer and Son Repairs* on the right side and a name tag on the left: *Magnar*. Looks like Mag is skipping off his weekend job early ... with a friend. A girl with fake-tomato-red hair skips down to the bay with Mag following behind. When they reach the dock, Elvy, Alessia, and I stand up from the bench and move to the bay.

Calynn was in this car. With this guy. At Opa's mailbox.

A few people are fishing at the far end of the long dock. You'd think there'd be good fishing from people walking so far out, but in all the years we've been coming to the ice-cream factory, and with all the people I've seen fishing, I've never actually seen anyone catch a fish. I'm hoping to catch a thief. I bet Mag was with Calynn when she went to Opa's, and he stole the letters. We sit down at a picnic table and watch.

On the dock, Mag tries to lick the fake redheaded girl's boring vanilla ice cream, but she snatches it away, giggles, then licks his face. We all say "Ew" at the same time, which is not good, because they look over at us and laugh. Mag does a double-take seeing Alessia, then nods a hello, probably recognizing her from her solo crime-scene investigation and photo shoot. The fake redheaded girl licks his face again, like it's better with an audience. It's not.

"Your cousins are little peeping Toms, aren't they?" she says. Cousins? Why would she call us his cousins? She giggles and playfully pushes him, but Mag loses his balance and grabs the fake redhead's arm really hard to stop from falling off the dock and into the bay.

"Don't ever do that again!" he yells, not playfully.

"Sorry, baby. I was just having some fun."

"Falling in the water is not fun. Got it?" he growls. Falling *near* the water is not fun either, I think, flashing on Calynn at Opa's shore. The fake redhead nods like a child in trouble with a parent: real quick, with eyes to the ground. She kisses him again, but all that gross love seems to be gone.

We walk back to the car and I lean against the hood, licking my ice cream. Mag notices and jogs up the rocky slope.

"I just got this baby cleaned, buddy. If you want to enjoy it, you can do it from there." He nods at the bench. Alessia and Elvy move away from the car and sit.

"I like it better over here," I say, and drop the rest of my cone on the hood of the car. The ice cream melts on contact with the heat of the hood and slides right off, leaving a nice long gooey smear of chocolate and brownie bits.

"What the hell! Get off my car, kid." He isn't smiling anymore. Why would he be? A family of four holding their cones makes a wide circle around us and heads to the dock, a little boy with chocolate ice cream all over his face walking backwards to watch us as he goes. His father hustles to turn him back around.

"First, Mag, why were you and Calynn Kearney at my grandfather's house?" I'm not sure where this sudden confidence is coming from. Curiosity? Anger? Ice cream brain freeze? I'm going with anger. I want answers. Even if the guy's double my size and bulging with muscles I didn't know existed. Even if my insides are shaking and the ice cream I did eat is making me feel like throwing up.

He looks down at his shirt to see his own name, like maybe he wasn't sure if that was him or not, and then smiles a very evil-looking smile—eyes narrowed, lips tight, like the Grinch when he's planning to steal Christmas.

"Why were you and Calynn Kearney at my grandfather's house?" I say again.

All I get is a stone face, not even a flicker in the eyes.

"What did you do to Calynn?" A sudden burst of cow smell takes over the sweet ice-cream air, along with an appropriately loud *moo*.

"Calynn fell on your grandfather's crappy stairs and busted her neck."

I scrunch my face just a bit at another flash of Calynn, her image permanently etched in my brain. I shake my head to shake away the image. But it'll be back. It always comes back.

"So you were there. You know she fell. You know the stairs were bad."

"It was in the paper, and I'm the one who fixed the stairs. Now get off my car."

That's right. It was in Alessia's laminated copy. Think. Think. "Well, you sure seem upset about Calynn's death. How long before you found *her*?" I jut my chin in the direction of the fake redhead, standing by the corner of the ice-cream factory, just enough to hear, but far enough away to stay out of the conversation. "What were you doing at my grandfather's house?"

"Fixing his stairs," he says, all cool, like he's done this before.

Has he done this before? Is Mag the local man who was brought in for questioning?

"Yeah, a little too late. But I'm talking before that."

"Putting in railings."

"No, the time you were there with Calynn."

Mag squints as the sun's rays hit him full-on, the clouds moving as quickly as all the theories in my head. He doesn't stop squinting, sneering at me, while he's trying to figure out how to answer.

“I have no idea what you’re talking about,” Mag says over a chorus of moos from the barn.

My eyes narrow as I try to read him. “I don’t believe you.”

“I don’t care.” He moves to the driver’s side door, but I block him by leaning against it. “Kid, I don’t want to hurt you.” A couple slips past the car with their cones, not giving us a second glance.

“Like you hurt Calynn? Where are the letters?” I try to hold my voice steady.

“What letters?” He holds his voice steady, too.

“The ones she went to get for my grandfather, the ones you stole. The ones with the old stamps.” Is this how detectives work? Do they just say whatever comes to mind and hope the person they’re talking to has no idea that you have no idea what you’re talking about? Because that’s what’s going on here. I really have no idea if he took the missing letters with the stamps or if he was even with Calynn the day she died. But he was with her in this car a month before. It’s possible.

“You drove her to my grandfather’s house and saw what was in the strongbox. Your family knows all about stamps; they sponsor that show that’s coming up next week. You saw the letters, saw the stamps, had a hunch they were valuable, and took them for yourself. Calynn didn't like that you were stealing from her grandfather's friend. She grabbed the letters from you, ran out of the garage, and you chased her to get them back."

I keep going, my voice steady now without even trying. He's standing there smirking, like he's above all of this. "She ran toward the cliff, you followed. All she could do was go down, so she took her chances and broke through the danger tape across the top of the stairs. You kept running after her and, when you caught up to her, you pushed her down the stairs, grabbed the letters, and left."

"I didn't push her."

I freeze. My mouth drops open. I stare at Mag. "That's the only thing I got wrong?" I say this more like a statement than a question.

He's definitely not smirking anymore. Part shock, part horror takes over his face. A crazed look—one eye almost closed, his nose wrinkled up, one cheek going in and out like maybe he's chewing on it. His body doesn't move, but his car keys dangle from his pinkie.

"How could you just leave her there? Maybe she would have lived if you'd rushed her to a hospital or called an ambulance."

Nothing. Not one word. Not one move. Not one regret.

"Where are the letters?" I try to open the driver's side

door. Now he's moving. His massive hands shove me to the ground. I fall like I'm on the soccer field, taking a step before collapsing forward, safely, and bounce back up just as quickly as if I was in the middle of a game.

"Leave my brother alone!" Elvy screams. With a quick glance, I see Alessia holding her back, but Elvy struggling to pull away, like she's ready to take on Mag herself. Not a good idea. I shouldn't even be taking him on, but I can't stop now.

I rush to the other side of the car to open that door, but he's on me, his tree-trunk arms grabbing my waist that I'm sure he could crush in one move. He spins me, my lanky legs flailing, and throws me toward the back end of the car.

"HOOOOOONK!" A lady in a big black pickup truck and big brown cowboy hat slams on her brakes. I know because I can hear the tires make that I-can't-stop-this-quickly squeal.

"Ruffians! This is a parking lot. If you want to roughhouse, go to the park!" she yells and then peels away. I close my eyes as bits of rock and debris hit me in the face.

Sirens in the distance. Louder and louder. Closer and closer. Until they're blaring and flashing right behind the teeny tiny yellow car.

The doors on either side open and slam.

"Magnar Geyer, you are under arrest for ..." one cop begins. I collapse to the ground, not hearing the rest of what she says. Elvy runs over and covers me with kisses. Ew.

The other cop nods to a woman with two very long braids and a white-and-black Milky Way Bay baseball cap, standing by the store door. The owner. She must have called the police. The same officer gives me a hand and helps me onto the bench, Elvy still clinging to me. Alessia puts an arm around my shoulders.

"You okay?" the cop asks, kneeling in front of me.

I nod.

"How about you two?" he asks Elvy and Alessia. They nod, too.

"Thanks for the call yesterday," he whispers to me.

"Did I figure out the motive? Did I solve the case?" I ask, my breath all puffy.

"You were a big help." He pats my knee, smiles, and joins his partner in the squad car. They take off, one person extra.

Elvy wraps her arms around my neck. Normally, I'd jerk away, but I don't. I don't think I'd get too far, anyway. Her hug is like a vice grip. She tells me I'm very brave. I think about Toots Meretsky, how he helped people by delivering those letters. Did I help Calynn by trying to find Opa's letters? Did I help Opa by proving that Calynn's death isn't his fault?

I'm shaking on the outside now. With Mag gone, just how terrified I was starts showing. I wonder if Toots Meretsky was terrified. How could he not have been? I was only up against Mag. He was up against the Nazis.

"It's time to go," I say, wobbling as I stand.

"Do you want another ice cream?" Elvy asks, her hand taking mine. I squeeze it and don't let go.

"Nah, Elvy, I've had enough."

Alessia, Elvy, and I grab our bikes and pedal home.

CHAPTER 18

Sunday, June 29 – Prince Edward County

"What are you doing?" I ask Elvy as the screen door slams behind me. I'm holding a glass of chocolate milk and trying to decide what to do with my day. I'm thinking about building that treehouse Opa never got around to. But I have no idea how to actually build a treehouse. Opa is the architect. Was, I guess. I'm a soccer player. Was, I guess. It's been four days since the last game. Four days since I quit. Four days since I touched a soccer ball. Four days since I've kicked, thrown, tapped, megged, dribbled, defended, passed, shielded, cupped, faked, crossed, shot, volleyed, tackled, scooped, blocked, deflected, jumped. Played.

I'm fine.

"I'm practicing." Elvy has a small popup net set up

by Opa's house and is kicking her ridiculous purple-and-pink zebra-stripe soccer ball into it. That ball is an embarrassment to the sport.

"You're in house league."

"I want to be as good as you." She smiles, then runs to the net to get her ball, her ponytail swinging from side to side, and gets ready to kick.

"Did Mom make you do this?" I see a cover-up all over that sweet smile. A plot.

"Make me do what?" She kicks and runs to the net.

"Make you set up that net and play to make me jealous or something, because it's not going to work."

"Wow. The world doesn't revolve around you, Liam. Why can't I practice?"

"Because I quit." I really want to get the ball and kick it to her, play with her, but I don't. I won't.

"So just because you made a dumb decision, I can't play anymore?" She holds the ball against her side and puts her hand on a jutted-out hip.

"No. Have fun." I walk along the mouse-colored porch and sit at the very end, overlooking the lake. No military planes blocking out the sound of the water lapping against the shore. Just the electric buzzing of a cicada and the ch-ch-ch of a chipmunk scurrying past. I lie on my stomach and look down over the edge, through the cedars and leaves of the oaks that have gotten so big, they block chunks of the black water so far down the cliff. From this spot, I can see the top of our jumping rock piercing like an iceberg, the masts of the sailboats catching the whipping wind, and the boats blasting across the lake at forty-five-degree angles. If Calynn had died on a day like today, her body probably would have been washed away into the lake by the waves. I would never have seen her. No one would ever have known what happened to her. The sun's rays set a spotlight on two kayakers in juicy orange life vests, cutting through the white-capped waves. Tough day to be paddling. One of the kayakers raises his paddle to say hello. I wave back. I want to go down to the water, but I don't. I won't.

I haven't been down to the shore since finding Calynn. It's not like I've needed to or anything. Alessia did the investigation there, so no need for me to do one, too. Mom and Elvy keep bugging me to go swimming and kayaking. I keep telling them I don't feel like it, even if it is crazy hot. I just don't want to.

"Liam!" Elvy shrieks like she's seen a dead mouse. No, wait, that's me. Ha, ha. I casually walk back to where she was playing, my heart panging as I see her stupid net.

"The ball went over the cliff!"

"So, what do you want me to do about it?" I start back for the porch. She grabs my hand.

"Can we see if it fell all the way down, please? It's my favorite ball."

"It's your only ball."

"Please!"

"No."

"But I can't go alone."

"I'm not going down there, not for you, not for anything."

At first, I think she's going to cry, her bottom lip all trembly. She stares at me, forcing me to look uncomfortably to the ground. There's a very small frog, no bigger than the size of my thumb, sitting about a foot away. I crouch down to pick it up. It doesn't jump away. I put it on my palm and it looks at me curiously. I stroke its back.

"I'll go with you. Please, Liam," she says softly.

"I don't want to."

She strokes the frog and then takes my other hand. "You're fine."

I take a deep breath. We walk to the top of the stairs, the frog happily coming along for the ride. With each foot forward, my legs put up a fight. I stop a moment, then step onto the long wood bridge that takes us to the first set of steps. Slimy. Slick. Step, step, step. As we make the turn, a few small stones slip from under my feet, and I shakily grab for a tree branch to keep my balance. We walk the short rocky path and look up at the cliff. We can't see her ball in the soccer ball graveyard, so we keep heading toward the water. As we get to the last set of steps, I freeze. Last set. Last step. Last breath.

The steps are different. New. Repaired by the guy who's been arrested for Calynn's death. We haven't heard anything else. I still have questions. Why did she run to the water? Does Mag have the letters? Will we ever get the stamps back? I put the frog on my shoulder and my hands on either rail. I don't want to go any further. I don't want to walk over the step that caused Calynn to die. Even if that step's not here anymore.

"Just a few more," Elvy says softly from behind me. Images swirl in my head; emotions swirl in the rest of me. Elvy puts her hands on my waist. I take another deep breath, try to keep it slow and steady. It comes out fast and choppy. We make it down to the cobblestone beach.

I stare at the spot where I found Calynn. You'd never know she was here once upon a time. Lying so still. So quiet. So dead. I shudder at the image still lasered in my brain, but I don't feel as sick as I was on the way down, not as sick as I thought I would be, being on the beach, staring at the spot. Not as sick as I've felt since the last time I was down here. With Calynn. Maybe because Mag was arrested. Maybe because I helped. I hope I helped.

I kick the stones a bit, as if moving them would uncover something to make sense of it all. Just stones and more stones. I pick up a perfect one to skip, loop my finger around it, and throw. One. Two. Three. Four. *Plunk.* I look for another. Find a fossil with a swirly pattern—a snail maybe—shove it in my shorts pocket.

Elvy moves around me and runs to her precious soccer ball.

"Liam! It's here. And so is another one! Goal!" She doesn't raise her hands and high-five nonexistent teammates. I take one more look at the spot, Calynn's spot, Opa's rock-skipping spot, and walk over to Elvy to see what got knocked loose. My German national ball, black, red, and white, with plenty of sticky tree sap and slime. I take it to the water to clean it off. The water's pretty cold. Not so much you can't go in, but enough that I'm happy with just my hands getting wet. Clusters of bubbles float on the surface of the water, whooshing when it washes against the shore. I put the frog down on one of the dry rocks. The wet ones are slimy with algae, and I can see zebra mussels clinging to them. Opa always warns us to wear water shoes, or the sharp shells will slit our feet open.

A ribbon of some sort is stuck to my Germany ball because of all the sap. It's got five stripes: one thick black one in the middle, two thin white ones on either side, and two thin red ones at the edges. The white is kind of yellowed now, but I don't think it's from being stuck in the soccer ball graveyard. It looks like one of those tea towels Opa has, that have yellowed with time, Mom would say. I would say they look like pee and won't touch them. The ribbon's a little frayed at the top and bottom, too. What is it and how did it get on the cliff?

"Liam."

I look up at Elvy, hugging her ball.

"Are you ready to go back up?"

"Yeah." I look at the ribbon. Maybe I found a treasure, like brewer's yeast and seeds left behind in a farmer's field.

CHAPTER 19

Monday, June 30 – Toronto

I shuffle and sprint down the brightly lit, disinfectant-smelling hallway to ask Opa about the ribbon. I slip into the hospital room. It's dark. Not the room exactly, but the life. Yeah, the life is dark.

Mr. Gargler raises a shaky hand to greet me. Just a shaky hand. The rest of his arm doesn't move.

Mr. Snorer isn't in his bed. Neither are his blankets or sheets.

Nausea churns in my gut and creeps up toward my throat. This room is haunted by all stages of death. I want to turn around but I don't. I won't. I want to know about the ribbon. I don't know why I think Opa'd know what it is, but I do. I walk straight to Opa's television and turn on the game. I can hear it perfectly without Mr. Snorer and his TV.

No explosions, gunfights, musical numbers, clashing and clanging metal. No silent movie. The ridiculous silent movie.

It's too quiet.

"*Mein Prinz*?" Opa croaks.

"Yeah, Opa, hi. Germany versus Algeria today." I try not to look at him. At his hollow face. At his sunken eyes. At his wrinkled skin. He looks like one of those gloom and doom pictures at his house, like the one that has a woman sitting and a kid standing over a man in a hospital bed.

"Ah ..." He breathes out heavily.

"A guy was arrested for Calynn's death," I say, staring at the television.

"Yes, I was told," he says, the words a whispery breath. "*Das is gut*."

"Opa." I get to the point. "I found something on the cliff." I pull the red, white, and black striped ribbon from my jeans and hold it in front of his unfocusing eyes. The sun, streaming through the window, blinds him, washes him out. I like the light, the not-dark, but I walk around the bed, adjust the blind, and hold up the ribbon again.

The ends of his mouth move up just enough to show a smile. Opa's trying to move his hand, but he's tucked in real tight, like a caterpillar in a cocoon. Except a caterpillar's cocoon is fat and healthy. Opa's cocoon is skeletal and sickly.

I pull away some of the blanket and cup the ribbon in his papery hand, so cold it gives me the shivers. He puts his hand on his chest, on his heart. I sit down, prop my feet on the corner of the bed, stare at the TV, and bite my bottom lip. The nausea churns faster and constricts my throat. I try to breathe in deep, but it's all gaspy.

"*Das Kriegsver … dienstkreuz.*"

"I don't know what that means, Opa." It sounds like a whole bunch of words stuck together. Which is what most German words sound like.

"The war merit … cross. An award … for bravery." Opa's other hand moves under the covers and then his whole arm falls limp over the side. I rush back over and raise the head of the bed for him, then put his arm back in its cocoon. The ribbon means something to him. That's good. That's really good.

"November 1943. I am not yet a soldier. The dark sky sparkles … like fireworks. But they are not fireworks. Our home shakes … My bedroom window shatters. Our door flies off its hinges. Mother and I … we run to the air-raid cellar, overcrowded. But we must remain. Hundreds of bombers flying overhead, hundreds and hundreds of bombs ... dropping without end. The reverberations ... from the explosions ... one pregnant woman gives birth. Right there."

Opa starts coughing. I fill a glass of water. Bring it to his lips. He doesn't sip.

"The artist Käthe Kollwitz lived ... down the street. She doesn't anymore. Do you know Käthe?"

Another weird turn. I don't need an art lesson from a thousand years ago. I need to know about the ribbon.

"No, Opa. What about the rib—"

"Do you know any artists?" He manages a mischievous smile. That's good. More life. Less dark. I bite.

"Pi-cas-so?"

"Do you like him?" Opa coughs. I bring the glass of water to his lips. No sips.

"No, creeps me out. All those twisted faces, with the eyes and ears and mouths in the wrong places." Creepy like the pictures in his house, but less death-staring-you-in-the-face.

"Ah ... so you learned something ... in school?" His smile gets bigger. Like he caught me. He wants me to like school. Like his schoolteacher father did. Like Opa must have, since he had to practically start all over again to become an architect when he came to Canada. He wasn't going to let the war get in the way of his dream.

His speech gets better as he speaks. Conversation is good. But it's not the conversation I want.

"I guess so. I won't do it again. Promise."

He tries to laugh. Tries to. More coughs. More water to lips. Still no sips. I open the drawer of the side table to grab a paper towel. All the Popsicle sticks and jams and margarines are gone. I wet the paper towel and drip some water onto his dried-out lips.

"Opa, can you tell me about the—"

"Frau Kollwitz draws our pictures when we visit her husband, the doctor. We visit often. Werner is always sick. Vials of poison."

This is making no sense. No ribbon and no sense. Wait, did he just say poison?

"Uncle Werner drank vials of poison?!" I didn't realize they just gave that stuff out. And to kids.

"*Nein ... nein*. The Kollwitzes carried them."

I let out a long, choppy sigh. That makes more sense. I guess. Not really. I pull my head from side to side to crack my neck. I need answers but I don't know how to get them. Machines buzz and beep in the hallway; visitors chit-chat and scuttle past on their way to see their dying person; the soccer game is on but it's all background noise to the questions pounding in my brain.

"They threaten to send her to a concentration camp … because her art is anti-war."

I can't imagine an artist being sent to a concentration camp just because her art is anti-war. But then I can't imagine my great-grandfather being sent to a concentration camp just because he corrected some eleven-year-old kid, or anyone being sent to a concentration camp just because they're Jewish or gay or Roma or whatever or whoever Hitler didn't like.

"Bombers are deafening," Opa goes on in a faraway whisper, talking like he's there, experiencing the war all over again.

A calm but determined voice calls out over the intercom with a code blue. Emergency. Medical people scramble past Opa's door. Opa won't get a code blue. He's here to die, not live. I swallow and can't help but wonder when that might be. Opa's fading. In color. In body. In mind. In voice. The doctor said he'd make it to the end of the World Cup, but not my birthday. That means two to eight weeks. In two to eight weeks, Opa will disappear forever. I wipe the frayed sleeve of my black Dortmund sweatshirt against my eyes.

"Opa, what's all this got to do with the ribbon?" I try again.

"They drone overhead without stop. But we aren't allowed to leave our homes, our cellars. We sit for a long time. I don't know how long. Me. My mother. Others from our building. The baby. When the planes die down and the all-clear sounds, I run outside. The sky is blood-red." Opa closes his eyes.

I close mine, too, and imagine a blood-red sky. A blood-red mouse. A blood-red Cougars' tank top. Death is everywhere. I have to stay focused on the ribbon. I look at Opa. His eyes are still closed.

"Opa?" I gently rock his shoulder. Nothing. My stomach drops. I rock harder. "Opa!"

"*Mein Prinz*?" His eyes flutter open. Coughs. Paper towel drips to lips.

"What happened after you left your building?" I ask. I want at least one question answered today. This one seems possible.

"The air is thick with smoke from the fires, as far as the eye can see. I find a piece of cloth and tie it around my nose and mouth ... to filter the smoke, block the stench, as I survey the damage. Shards of glass from windows glitter on the street like snow, crunch under my shoes. Doors balance like seesaws. The building the Kollwitzes once lived in is destroyed. A monstrous mound of brick and mortar and debris. From somewhere, the crackling of timber, trees. Yet everything is still, stunned. I hear wailing, but I don't see anyone. I climb on the pile of smoking rubble, steadying myself on my hands and knees, and follow the cries. I see a hand twitching and I dig as quickly as I can, throwing aside whatever I can lift. When the woman is uncovered, I pull, and the cries get even higher. She is a tangle of blonde hair, blackened by soot, and she aches everywhere, but she is out of the rubble. Others nearby carefully carry her away. The wailing continues, but it's lower, deeper. I crawl some more on the pile of people's former homes, close my eyes to hear better, crawl and repeat, until I think I know where the voice is coming from. I dig again. I find one foot, then another. They are pointing in opposite directions. I dig and dig and finally pull at the man, but he won't come free. He is clutching a young girl, maybe nine or ten. Many children had been evacuated from Berlin, but here she is. Here I am. I try to take her, tell the man I have her, and he lets go. Then I pull him out. His eyes are shut together with blood, but he can feel the breeze on his ashen face. He speaks to the child, tells her they're going to be okay." Opa closes his eyes again. "She does not answer."

A burst of cheering from the TV fills the room. I keep my eyes on Opa, smaller than ever. Larger than ever.

"So you're a hero," I whisper.

Opa has always just been an old man to me. A retired architect living in the countryside, building things at his house, swimming in the lake, playing with his grandchildren. Me. Elvy. I never imagined him as a teenager, living in a big city, able to save people from a bombed-out building. A hero.

"Saving a person does not make one ... a hero. Just a human being. If you can help another ... in any way ... you help." His breath is heavier again, his speech choppier. His eyes startle open with another round of explosive cheering. The sportscasters are talking at warp speed and just as loudly. It almost feels like Mr. Snorer is back in the room. Almost.

"You said it was a war merit *cross*. This is only a ribbon."

"I threw the cross out after I received it." He rolls his head to face me. He has a hard time focusing again, but when he does, I feel like he's studying me. I don't know what he wants to learn. He turns back to the television, then the window. There's nothing different to see. Every day has been sunnier than the last. No wind, few clouds, no rain. No change.

"The cross had a swastika. In the darkest days of the war, Hitler needed to keep up people's morale. I sure as hell didn't save my neighbors for Hitler. But I was proud ... to be recognized for bravery. The ribbon is enough to remember ... when I once did a brave thing."

I think about Toots Meretsky, about how Opa believed all Canadians were brave. Opa is brave. He is a brave Canadian. *If you can help another in any way, you help*, I repeat to myself. *If you can help another in any way...* Oh God. Oh God. I have a question for Opa that I don't want to ask. But I have to. Because if not now, then when?

"Opa." I shift uncomfortably in my chair, drop my feet to the floor, and look at his bony face. "You know, in all the stories you've told me, you never once ... well, you never once ... mentioned the Holocaust. You almost make it sound like it wasn't a part of the war, like it never happened. Don't you believe it happened?"

He rolls his head toward me, sees me, registers I'm here. But then his focus moves past me, on something behind me. I turn around. Mr. Gargler is watching Opa. Eyes I've never seen on him before. Curious. Cautious. Haunted.

"Oh, *mein Prinz*, of course the Holocaust happened. I only share with you my story, my experience ... For such accounts, you must speak to those who lived through that horror."

Mr. Gargler shifts his eyes to me. A cold breeze, like ghosts in the room, chills me. My eyes make their way along the arm Mr. Gargler always waves to me with.

A tattoo.

Of numbers.

My eyes sting and my nose tingles. The nausea rips at my insides like a storm on the cliff. I don't know what to do. I don't know what to say. I just sit. And stare. And think. And cry.

I'm not fine. I'm not fine at all. All this time, I never noticed, I never knew, I never asked.

I'll never forget.

"You are correct. I did not help," Opa says.

I slowly turn back to Opa, pulling my wet, burning eyes away from the numbers. The horrible, horrible numbers.

A tear rolls down his cheek and onto his pillow. "My silence kept me safe. My silence killed so many."

"You were only a kid," I whisper, my voice gaspy. Opa wasn't much older than me.

"I still had a voice," he says quietly.

If I was in his place, would I have saved people from a burning building? Would I have stood up and spoken out about my neighbors being taken away? Alessia is standing up and speaking out, with her book list that's going to the school board. It's easy to think I would do the right thing. But would I? I've never said anything when I've heard the n-word in school, didn't even realize how it made Alessia feel.

"Opa, what was the ribbon doing on the cliff?" I whisper.

He clenches the ribbon, then rolls his head toward the television. "Calynn was a brave girl," he says.

Calynn? Calynn died for a ribbon ... that Opa got for saving lives?

I rub my sweatshirt sleeve against my entire face, water stains making the black blacker. I don't want Opa to see me cry. I don't want to make him sad. Sadder. I turn back to the TV, to the game we haven't watched. I sniffle hard and rub my eyes again.

"You and Elvy are everything to me, *mein Prinz*. Everything."

I jump out of my chair and hug Opa real hard. "I'm glad I could find the ribbon for you."

He kisses my hair and rests his cold cheek on the top of my head. Maybe a German grandfather's undying love for his Jewish grandson is all the answer I need.

CHAPTER 20

Thursday, July 3 – Prince Edward County

Last night was the first soccer game I didn't play. Didn't even watch my teammates play. I haven't heard how it went, and I don't think I want to know. It's over. Isn't that what Coach always said: *You keep thinking about the past, you're not going to have a future*? That's what everyone keeps saying about everything. Mom. Dad. The therapist.

Not Opa.

All he does is talk about the past. All those horrible stories. They make quitting soccer seem pretty unimportant. I have to move on. To what, I have no idea. I don't know anything else but soccer. That was my thing. Mine and Opa's thing.

"Big article today," Dad says as he sits down with the County paper, not laminated. I grab some chocolate milk out of the puke-green fridge and sit by Dad as he reads out loud to me, Elvy, and Mom.

"The former boyfriend of the late teen found dead along Lake Ontario in Prince Edward County in May was arrested Sunday.

"Magnar Geyer, 18, of Picton, has been charged with criminal negligence in the death of Calynn Kearney, 17, also of Picton, confirmed an officer with the Prince Edward County Detachment of the Ontario Provincial Police.

"When Miss Kearney didn't return from her regular afternoon run on Friday, May 30, her parents reported her missing. The next day, the OPP was called to the home of Prince Edward County resident Friedrich Reimold, who at the time was—and remains—in hospital in Toronto. Upon confirming the body to be that of Miss Kearney, police announced the missing persons case closed. As to the cause of death, Miss Kearney had broken through a rotten step along the cliff and fell down the stairs, resulting in a cervical spine fracture. Police, however, suspected foul play and ruled out the possibility of an accident."

Missing persons. Case closed. Rotten step. Cervical spine fracture. Accident. The words I heard the day I found Calynn.

"Mr. Geyer had been dating Miss Kearney for over a month, but the Kearney family says they were not aware of the relationship. The officer would not reveal why Miss Kearney and Mr. Geyer were at the Reimold home, but did say that the trip set off a chain of events that directly led to Miss Kearney's death."

He offered to drive her so she could pick up the ribbon from the strongbox. He saw the letters with the old stamps and tried to steal them. Stupid stamps. Calynn and Uncle Werner killed for the same reason. *When you're desperate, you do what you can to stay alive. It doesn't always make sense, your choices.* Opa said that about Werner and his so-called friends. Calynn should have run to the road but, for some reason, she ran to the water.

Not for some reason.

"Because he can't swim," I say quietly.

Dad looks up from the newspaper. "Who can't swim?"

"Magnar Geyer. That's why Calynn ran to the water. There's never anyone on the road; she'd never have gotten any help. But when the fake redhead at the ice-cream factory nearly pushed Mag into the lake, he freaked out.

My guess is because he can't swim and Calynn could. She grabbed the letters he wanted to steal, and she tried to get away from him. She must have thought the lake was her best chance."

Dad starts reading again. *"The police were on their way to Mr. Geyer's home Sunday afternoon, when an altercation between Mr. Geyer and a male youth at the Milky Way Bay ice cream factory was reported by the owner."*

Mom and Dad look at me. I smile awkwardly and shrug my shoulders. "You shouldn't have locked us out of the house and blackmailed us with twenty bucks."

"Bribery, not blackmail," Mom explains. Still illegal.

"The OPP took Mr. Geyer into custody at Milky Way Bay. Mr. Geyer has also been charged with theft, trespassing, and breaking and entering."

"He was bringing girls into the house," I say.

"I think the reporter is referring to the property and the garage. No mention of the house," Dad says as he scans the rest of the article.

"He was in the house. Remember, Elvy? The fake redheaded girl at the ice-cream factory thought we were Mag's cousins, which means she's seen us before." I jut my chin at the photos over the fireplace. "He probably told her we were related when he brought her here and she saw our school pictures."

I feel like Sherlock. Not the heavy frustration with people who can't keep up, but the big reveal based on tiny clues. *Watch and learn.* That advice from Coach was bang on. Elvy nods at what I'm saying, like my very own Dr. Watson.

"That's why my stuffies were out of place on the sofa. Because he came inside and moved them." Elvy squeezes the stuffed bear on her lap.

"And why the curtains were open," I add. "Calynn would've told Mag that Opa wasn't living here anymore when she mentioned the ribbon. He probably offered to help since he had the lockbox combination from when he and his dad put in the handrails, before Opa got sick. So they drove here, unlocked the house, and grabbed the garage key. I mean, it hangs right by the front door." I point to the rack of numbered keys.

Elvy leans forward, with one side of her face scrunched up like she's thinking hard. "And then he decided he could use the house because he figured no one else was."

Mom and Dad look confused. Or amazed. Or both.

"Exactly," I keep going. "He wouldn't have used the house with Calynn because, well, she died, but with the redhead, for sure. Wouldn't that be a teenage guy's dream, his own hangout away from his parents?" I can't understand how he could come back here. I mean, I've heard criminals return to the scene of the crime, but why?

Mom and Dad grimace at the thought of strangers here. I bet Mom's going to sterilize the whole house.

"If he could get into the house, why wouldn't he steal something else, like the TV or the stereo?" Elvy asks.

I look at the TV. It's a huge square box, the kind of thing people in Toronto lug to their front lawns and dump, hoping someone will take it away. The stereo is so ancient it has a tape player, and the speakers are taller than Elvy. I'm no expert, but I don't think any of this stuff is worth stealing. Who'd want it? Old stamps, though, if someone like Mag had a hunch they could be valuable, then maybe they'd be worth the risk. And anyway, if he stole the TV, he'd have nothing to watch when he hung out here.

A loud knock makes us jump. Dad opens the door and finds two cops standing out front.

"I see you've read the news," the first one says, glancing at the paper in Dad's hand. Dad nods and invites them in. The second cop puts photos of Opa's stolen letters on the coffee table.

"Where are the actual letters?" I ask.

"We need them a little longer," he says. "We'll get them back to you. Promise." I nod. What else can I do?

Dad moves the photos around on the table, leaning in close to examine each envelope. "These are old letters from Germany addressed to my father, but they're not from Werner," Dad says when he sits back up. He collects the photos and hands them back. "The return address isn't Werner's and the postmarks aren't from Berlin."

"Mag must still have them, then," I say. "We need them back before he soaks the stamps and finds the valuable ones underneath. Opa said that's how Werner sent them and that's how to get them."

"Those are the only letters we found," the second cop says, moving to the front door and checking out the hanging lockbox. "Maybe the letters you're looking for are still here in the house. Or maybe your grandfather already soaked them and sold them."

Opa didn't sell them. He wouldn't. They're all he has left of his brother.

"I don't know much about stamps," the first cop says, "but are used stamps even worth much?"

"They're worth Uncle Werner's life," I say. "And Calynn's."

She nods and smiles sadly, like Doctor Burakgazi that

day we talked about Opa's cancer. Happy and unhappy that I understand. "You're right, kid."

If the stamps aren't with these letters, if they weren't even in the strongbox, then Calynn died protecting nothing. *Many people are killed for no reason*, I hear Opa say. But it shouldn't be that way. The world shouldn't work that way.

"You should change your lockbox combo after every service call," the second cop says, letting the lockbox drop and bump against the door. "Slew of break-ins reported because of them."

I climb the rope ladder to the top bunk, lie down, and look at my posters on the ceiling. Opa's spent so much time telling me stories about his life. I know Werner really died young. I know my great-grandfather really disappeared. I know Oma really loved candy. The stamps have to be true, too. Weidenfeller. Lewandowski. Dortmund. Germany. Weidenfeller. Lewandowski. Dortmund. Germany. Weidenfeller. Lewandowski. Dortmund.

Germany.

I sit up, my head brushing the cedar-beamed ceiling, to look at Germany more closely. All the other posters are stuck with tape at the four corners. The German national team is taped all around. I peel off a corner, slowly, carefully.

As I pull the poster back, frosted envelopes the size of a cellphone fall onto my bed.

"Dad! Dad! Come quick!"

Elvy kicks the top bunk with her foot to make me know she is not amused. "I'm trying to sleep!" she yells from below, but rolls out of bed anyway and climbs up the rope ladder.

"What's going on?" Dad asks.

I hold up some of the envelopes. "I found the stamps in my sleep!"

"Why would he hide them?" Elvy asks as she hops onto my bed and looks through the designs—ships, planes, palm trees, eagles, faces, numbers, every color you can imagine.

Why *would* he hide them? It's not like they're illegal, like he's not allowed to have them. They belong to Opa. Uncle Werner sent them to him before he was killed. They're all Opa has left of his brother. I think about what Mom said about her Jewish identity, about when others thought she'd lose it marrying Dad. About how it actually made her feel stronger about it, more protective of it. Maybe when there's a risk of something being taken away, you hold on to it with all you've got.

"He hid them so he wouldn't lose his brother again."

CHAPTER 21

Friday, July 4 – Toronto

Dad's been driving back and forth between Toronto and the County, between Opa and us, all week. But it's the first day back for Mom, Elvy, and me since Monday, since the last Germany World Cup game. We always spend the first month after the end of school at Opa's. With Opa. It makes no sense being in the County without him, but Mom decided not to say anything, what with Dad needing his routine, needing to keep everything as normal as possible.

When we hit the outskirts of Toronto, Mom turns from the passenger seat and slips me an envelope with my name on it. It's from the Holocaust museum in the United States. After I told her about Opa's schoolteacher father disappearing forever, she told me this museum's been collecting information about survivors and victims and said I should give them a call.

"How long have you had this?" I ask. Elvy leans over to take a look, but loses interest while I stall, flipping the envelope in every direction.

"Montreal train!" she says, pointing out her window. Normally I'd look, but not this time. I'm fixated on what's in my hands.

"Not long." Mom says, not biting her bottom lip. I guess she's not worried about what I'll find inside. So why am I? I stare at my name.

"Toronto train! Two for one!" Elvy yells.

I rip open the top of the envelope and scan the letter. Sachsenhausen concentration camp. North of Berlin. My great-grandfather was taken there as a political prisoner, for criticizing the Nazis, because some jerk kid ratted him out. I don't want to read all the details right now. But I look for the date of death: 1941. July 4. Today.

My parents drop me at the Veterans Centre and say they'll go for lunch and be back for their own visit right after the game. Enough time for me to tell Opa about the stamps, and his father. Maybe it will help him to finally know.

I go through the same big hospital doors. Walk the same long hallway to the elevator. Check out the same warplane pictures and wave to the same veterans, still wearing their same berets and army caps. I press the same floor number and feel the same whoosh of the pulleys and ropes. When the elevator doors slide open, I zip past the same bright yellow lobby and brown leather chairs, and through the same heavy doors to the same machine-lined hallway. I turn the same corner. I walk through the same open door and smell the same disinfectant smell as I enter the same room.

"Germany versus France, Opa, are you ready?"

Opa is not here.

Everything is the same. But everything is different. Mr. Gargler is here. Only Mr. Gargler. He raises a few fingers to wave. Only a few fingers.

I drop my knapsack on the floor and run to the nurses' station.

"Where's my grandfather?" I ask. Three people behind the desk, and not one pays any attention to me. I say it louder. "Where's my grandfather?" A nurse I've never seen before finally turns around.

"Please do not yell. This is a hospital, not a schoolyard."

"Where is my grandfather?" I say again.

"What is his room number?" Room number? Are patients just room numbers?

"His name is Friedrich Reimold." She types his name into the computer.

"Wait just a moment, please." Where does she think I'm going to go? I see Doctor Burakgazi come out of the room next to Opa's, and I don't wait a second to grab him.

"Hey, champ." He's got the same voice, but he speaks different. He's got the same eyes, nose, mouth, ears, skin, but he looks different.

"Where's my grandfather?" He puts an arm around my shoulder and leads me to a room. A different room.

"I was about to call your parents," he says, and I know I don't want to hear anymore.

"You said he'd make it through the World Cup! You said so!"

He nods even though my fists are hitting him. My arms are cement. I can't lift them, but I'm somehow hitting the doctor. I'm hitting him in the chest. Over and over and over. I can't stop.

"The game starts in just a couple of minutes. I need Opa. It's the quarter finals. Do you understand? The quarter finals. Germany versus France. It's an important game. You said he'd make it! You said so!"

He takes my hands, puts them by my sides, and wraps me in a hug. The doctor is hugging me. He's hugging me, even though I was hitting him. I feel so heavy. So heavy, I sink to the floor.

From somewhere, I hear a whistle blow.

Opa has disappeared forever.

CHAPTER 22

Tuesday, July 8 – Prince Edward County

The ringing in my ears wouldn't quit. For three days, cellphones blared, text messages pinged, doorbells rang. When no one was calling Mom and Dad, Mom and Dad were getting in touch with the funeral home for the service and coffin, the cemetery for the burial plot, the transport service for bringing Opa back to the County from Toronto, friends and family for attending the funeral, blah, blah, blah.

Today, all the noise has stopped. Dead silence. Even Lake Ontario is mirror-still, no waves slapping the cliff, no croaking from the frogs, no wind rustling the leaves of the oak trees. A cormorant flies so low, I can see its reflection on the water.

At 3:30 PM, Mom comes to get me. I'm sitting at the

shore, right where I found Calynn, skipping stones on the water three ... four ... five.

"We have to leave for the funeral now," she says, sitting down on one of the new steps.

"The game's on in half an hour. I'm not going." I whip a rock into the lake, watch circles form and expand.

"It's your chance to say goodbye," she says quietly, calmly.

"No, it's not. It's a chance to watch Opa be lowered into the ground and suffocated in the earth." I whip another stone at the water. *Plunk*.

"It may help, to have some closure," she says, breathing deeply.

"Did it help you? When Zaidie died? Did you feel better watching him get buried? I saw you, at the funeral home. I saw you standing there, in the family room, alone, you staring at Zaidie in a box."

"I didn't know you—"

"I was quiet. I was coming to get you, and I saw you just standing there. With the box. I hid around the corner, and when you came out, you were crying. Did that help you? Are you better for seeing him in a box? Seeing him lowered into the ground?"

I hear her shift on the step, but she doesn't say anything. A single sniffle tells me she's thinking about Zaidie now.

Now, when she needs to be strong for everyone else.

"I went to Zaidie's funeral. And Oma's. I'm not doing it again." I pick up a handful of stones, thrown them all. *Plunk, plunk, plunk.*

"Are you sure?" She sniffles again.

"I have a game to watch."

"Okay." The stones crunch and scrape against one another as she walks over. She kisses me on the top of my head and walks up the stairs. When I hear the doors slam and the car pull out, I head up to the house. I turn the television on to find the channel for the game. Flick, flick, flick. The pre-game is on. Stats and history about the German and Brazilian teams. A win today means going to the finals. Germany hasn't won the World Cup since 1990. Brazil hasn't won since 2002 when they beat Germany, and since this World Cup is in Brazil, well, you can imagine how desperate they are to get to the finals. They won't.

The screen fills with the field now, the cheering gets all thunderous as the players come out and get into position. Weidenfeller's still not in goal. The starting whistle blows.

I turn off the TV.

"How was the game?" Alessia asks, tossing my sweatshirt off an armchair and at me, so she can sit down.

"It was okay." I'm lying on the sofa, staring at Opa's depressing wall of prints and posters. In some twisted way, looking at them makes me feel a little better.

"Who won?" Alessia asks, swinging a crossed leg back and forth.

"Germany." I'm guessing. I don't really know.

"What was the score?" she says with an annoying, sing-songy voice.

"Why are you here?" I don't take my eyes off the pictures.

She ignores the question and keeps talking. "I met Calynn's grandfather at the funeral. He talked about losing two special people in his life in so little time."

How could he and Opa have been so close and I've never met him? Or Calynn?

"Kane and Ryder cried during your dad's eulogy." I look over the sofa arm at Alessia, who's got one of those smiles that makes you think she was waiting for me to look at her, like she knew just what to say to make it happen, tight and wide with laughing eyes. She's got another book in her hands—during summer vacation. I glance at the title: *A Wish After Midnight*. Never heard of it. I wish Alessia would leave me alone, but I know that's not going to happen.

"Why were Ryder and Kane at the funeral?"

"Everyone was at the funeral," Alessia says.

I bite. "Everyone who?"

"Our class. They carpooled." She keeps swinging her leg.

Why would they come to my grandfather's funeral more than two hours away from Toronto? That's insane. They didn't even know him.

"They felt like they knew him," Alessia says, reading my mind. What in the world is that supposed to mean, *they felt like they knew him*? Leave it to Alessia to make a mystery out of nothing. And to investigate it herself. "From his school visits, soccer games, the letter he wrote to us with the answers about his time in the war. I told Ryder and Kane about the funeral, and I guess word got around."

I guess that makes sense. Kind of. Not really. "Where's everyone now?"

"They went back to Toronto. Ryder and Kane are staying at my place, so they're outside, playing soccer with Elvy. She's whipping them pretty badly."

"Such a waste of talent on house league," I mutter, looking back at the wall of gloom and doom. The screen door opens. Dad passes in front of me to the kitchen. I can hear Ryder, Kane, and Elvy playing—*oofs* and *bams* and *yays* and *oh come ons*—as the screen door closes.

"She has a good teacher."

"I've seen her coach—he sucks. Doesn't know the

difference between a free kick and a penalty kick. Elvy's had to explain it to him." I get up from the sofa and walk over to the wall, look at a small sketch in the corner by the fireplace.

Alessia continues. "You, Liam. You're the good teacher." From her no-nonsense tone, I know she rolled her eyes when she said that, like things have to be spelled out for me to get them. "You're a good big brother."

"What in the world is this?" Dad says from the kitchen.

"I'm trying," I say, ignoring Dad. Getting along with Elvy was one of Opa's orders the day we watched the Boateng brothers. Brothers—the sketch is of two brothers.

"Liam, can we talk?" Dad calls over.

"See you later, Liam," Alessia says. I don't turn to say goodbye. "By the way, Germany crushed Brazil seven to one. I think your grandfather would have liked that score."

An elbow jabs me in my side.

"Ow! What did you do that for?" I say, looking at Alessia and rubbing at the pain. She has strong elbows.

"Seemed like the right thing to do." She smiles and leaves. I smile too, a little. She's so weird.

"Your grandfather left you something," Dad calls again.

When I don't move, he comes over and taps me on the shoulder.

"I'll look at it later." I take the frame off the wall.

"I'd really like you to look at it now," he says, glancing at the picture.

"Do you know who they are?" I ask, holding the sketch so he can see it better.

"Kind of looks like your grandfather when he was a child," he says with a laugh.

It kind of does. I tilt the picture from side to side, the glass reflecting the sun just as much as a laminated piece of newspaper. It looks real, not like a print or poster. I turn it over and open the back.

"What are you doing?" Dad asks.

"Checking." It's not glossy paper like a poster would be, it's thicker, heavier, yellower. Was this in Opa's strongbox that he rescued from his building? It must have been. There's a message on the back. In German.

"*Für Friedrich und Werner, zwei wunderschöne Brüder. Käthe Kollwitz.* For Friedrich and Werner, two wonderful brothers. Opa really did know Käthe Kollwitz. Holy crap."

"Don't say crap. Who's Käthe Kollwitz?"

"You don't read enough." I grab the book about Käthe Kollwitz sitting on the shelf right below where the sketch was hanging. Right next to a book about the Nazi Olympics. And one about U-boats. And one about the Holocaust. And one about Jewish holidays. And one about German soccer. And one about choosing a coffin. Wait, what? I pull it out a bit—a short story collection. That makes more sense. I guess. Not really. I push it back in, pull out the soccer book, and toss it on the chair where Alessia was sitting. "I want this drawing in your will."

"Um ... okay. Since we're talking about giving you things, can you look at this thing your grandfather left you now?"

I follow Dad to the kitchen. On a chair is the white-and-blue file folder box Ryder had given me with the gifts for Opa. The hospital must have packed up Opa's stuff. In the middle of the table is an architectural model made from mini jam containers, Popsicle sticks, and, I'm assuming, school glue.

"The Olympiastadion," I whisper.

My dad leans over and looks at it closely.

"Opa was at the opening ceremony of the Olympic Games in 1936." I run back to the living room to grab the soccer book. Flip, flip, flip until I find a photo. There must be a photo. I grab the Nazi Olympics book and try again. Flip, flip, flip. There it is. I lay it on the kitchen table, then turn the structure around carefully, looking at the oval stadium, built from layers of mini containers of peanut butter, jam, and margarine. A gazillion Popsicle stick pillars go all the way around the stadium, up to the top. The containers and Popsicle sticks are painted white. The whole thing sits on what looks and feels like Opa's green bathrobe wrapped over some sort of strong board. Everything about the model is perfect. I don't understand how he could be so precise with this building when he could hardly hold a glass of water. Opa's built a lot of things in his life, but this has got to be the most impressive. I look inside. The seating is made from sloping containers making their way down to the center. I gasp. I actually gasp.

Dad looks at me with one eyebrow up, then looks inside. In the middle of the green-bathrobe field is a podium. On the highest podium, it says USA. On the lowest podium, it says Mexico. On the middle podium, it says Canada. Basketball. This was the basketball result at the 1936 Olympics. Each podium has the country's flag rising from it. But not Canada's. Canada's podium has a black, white, and red striped flag. Which is not a flag at all. It's the ribbon from Opa's war merit cross, his award for bravery.

"The ribbon was for me," I whisper-cry. "That's what Calynn came for. To get this for Opa. So he could give it to me. I'm the reason she's dead. I killed her! I killed her!"

I fly out of the kitchen and race out of the house. I run. Across the porch. Down the steps. Along the rocky ground. Through the forest. Over the grass. Onto the road. Past the wildflowers. Yellow. Purple. White. Blended together. Round the bend. Cows. In their field. Awful smell. Hear nothing. Only pounding. Pound, pound, pound. Feet. Head. Heart. No one on the road. No one ever on the road.

Except animals. Dead frogs. Run over by cottagers' big cars. Vultures feasting. Hear my footsteps. Scatter. Another noise. In the bush. Something watching. Hear that something bound away. Frightened rabbit. I reach an intersection. Stop. I bend over to catch my breath, but I can't. I can't breathe. She died because of me. She died so Opa could make me the Olympiastadion. That can't be the reason. That can't be the end of it. Of her. Of Calynn.

I fall onto the road's sandy shoulder. Pick up a handful of sand. Wet. From my tears. I spot a frog on the road. Belly up. I pick up a stick from the ground. Poke the body with the stick. Not a sound.

Except for Dad.

"Liam!"

Dad's running. I can barely see him through the wetness. I can hear him, though. His awkward breathing. Short. Like he doesn't run. He doesn't.

"Liam," he says again. Leaning over. Hands on knees. Breathing. Still awkwardly. Deeply. Wheezily. He drops onto the shoulder. Next to me.

"I'm the reason she's dead," I repeat the words. The awful words. The awful truth.

"No, Liam. You had absolutely nothing to do with Calynn's death. If she was trying to stop this guy from stealing from your grandfather, she didn't have to run with the letters. She didn't have to run to the water. She didn't have to run at all. She could have walked out of here and reported what happened to the police, and they could have dealt with it."

"So it's her own fault she's dead?"

"No, no, that's not what I'm saying. What I'm saying is it's not so simple."

"She was here because of Opa, because of me."

"No, not really. It sounds like she decided to save her grandfather a trip, but no one asked her. George told the police that Opa asked him to get the ribbon, and Opa told me. I looked for the ribbon but couldn't find it. He never actually told me what it was for, and I didn't know you knew about it."

"We haven't spent much time together since ..." I start sobbing again and lean into my dad.

"No, we haven't."

He hugs me tightly. So many thoughts run through my head. So many things I want to talk to him about, ask him about. "She fell at Opa's house. On his broken stairs. Is that illegal or something? Can we lose Opa's house? I don't want to lose Opa's house. I can't lose his house! I can't lose any more of him!" Dad wraps his arms around me. He doesn't say anything. I feel wetness on my head. Tears. Dad's crying. My dad's crying. I've never even asked him how he's doing. About Opa. Opa was his dad. His dad. Gone.

"Are you okay, Dad?" I squeak out.

"Yeah, kid. I'm fine." He squeezes me hard. I can't breathe. Big gasps as my tears start coming again. I try to slow my breathing. In. Out. In. Out. I focus on the dead frog. Flattened, like Berlin. Guts, blood speckled all over the road. *Killed for no reason.* In. Out. In. Out. *Never know when life will be taken away.* I play with the sand on the shoulder of the road with my free hand. Dig my fingers in. Dig. Dig. I loosen myself from Dad's grip. Dig. Dig. A hole. I look behind me. A piece of bark. I take it, and my stick. I scoop up the dead frog, take the frog off the road. Put it in the hole. Cover it up. Pat it down. Daisies just behind. *Disappeared forever.*

"I want to go home." I stand up and wipe my wet face with my dirty hands.

"You look like you're wearing war paint," Dad says, looking at the muddy streaks on my face, trying to make a joke.

"I hope I never have to fight in a war."

CHAPTER 23

Thursday, July 10 – Prince Edward County

"Liiiiiiiam. Where are you?"

I focus on the black and yellow soccer net. Try to ignore Elvy kicking up stones and making the dry moss crackle as she gets closer. I take a deep breath. I am Robert Lewandowski, top scorer in the Bundesliga.

"What are you doing?" she asks. She's petting a tiny frog in the palm of her hand. When she sees I'm getting ready to kick, she runs off toward the forest, then back and into the net.

"I'm practicing. Obviously. Where's the frog?" She points at the forest without taking her eyes off the ball. I steady my foot, pull back, and kick. The ball speeds toward Elvy and, for a minute, I think it's going to whack her in the face, but she moves to the right and grabs the ball with both hands.

"Save!" She drop-kicks the ball and high-fives her nonexistent teammates.

"Very funny," I say with a smirk. She really is good. She's a pretty good sister, too.

"I thought you quit."

"I did." I roll the ball onto my right foot and do keep-ups. "Coach called last night, asked if I was ready to come back." Four, five, six ...

Coach said she'd been thinking a lot about the last couple of months. She thought tough love would snap me back to normal more than all the touchy-feely therapist stuff. I told her maybe it would have, but when you dish out tough love all the time, it loses all meaning. It just becomes mean. And that's not what a coach is supposed to be. She listened and apologized. But said she was still going to wear her Bayern hat when I least expected it, to keep me on my game—and to remind me that Lewandowski left Dortmund at the end of this past season and signed with Bayern, which I've been trying to forget. Blech.

"Ryder told me they're sinking in the standings and that Marco quit. He couldn't take the pressure." Ten, eleven, twelve ... Birds are cawing to the beat of my keep-ups, or maybe it's the other way around. The oak trees rustle in the wind like a whispering audience in the stands. The old cedars don't move or make any noise at all, silent watchers.

"I think if they need you so badly, you should go on the condition she gets you your tryout with that elite team," Elvy says with the determination of a sports agent.

I smile, popping the ball on my right foot, then thigh, shoulder, head, shoulder, thigh, foot, thigh, shoulder, head ...

"Is your head back in the game?" she asks.

"Can't you tell?"

She groans.

"I don't think it ever left the game. At least, the game never left my head. Not really."

"So then shouldn't you be Weidenfeller and me Lewandowski?"

"You'll kick on me?" Foot, thigh, shoulder, head ...

"I need to practice. Even if it is just dumb house league."

"Thanks, Elvy."

"You won't be thanking me when I kick the hell out of the ball."

"You're not supposed to say hell," I say.

She shrugs, then whips her leg up and around toward my head and kicks the ball into the net. Such a waste.

We play for over an hour and then head back to the house, all sweaty and gross and starving. The door isn't locked, so we sneak in and raid the kitchen for lemonade, oranges, a package of cheese curds, and two boxes of crackers. We bring it all outside and sit at the very end of the mouse-colored porch overlooking the lake.

"Hey, Elvy," I say with a mouth full of crackers.

"Yeah?" she replies with a mouth full of cheese.

"We should go see a soccer game at the Olympiastadion together. When we're older, I mean." No need to spin a globe and put down a finger.

"Where's the Olympiastadion?"

"Berlin."

"But you like Dortmund."

"Then we'll go when Berlin is playing Dortmund." I peel an orange and bite into a section. Juice sprays all over my face.

"Won't you be playing for Dortmund by then?"

Huh. Will I? I look out at the lake. Lots of sailboats today, not really going anywhere, just enjoying a warm, sunny day. Voices carrying along the water. By evening, the sailboats won't be there. Moved on to their next destination. *Experience the world*, Opa said. I hope I'll be in Dortmund when I'm older. I also hope I'll be right here.

"Do you think we can get real German pretzels at the stadium, like the ones Dad tells us are junk?" Elvy shoves her hand in a cracker box and pulls out the largest handful she can handle.

"Probably, and I bet they'll be as big as your face! And then we can go to the neighborhoods where Oma and Opa grew up, and see where the Berlin Wall used to divide east and west, and visit the Käthe Kollwitz museum, and find where the candy bomber dropped his parachute parcels, and walk around the Jewish quarter, and go to the Berlin Zoo, and—" I cut myself off. I don't think I want to visit the Sachsenhausen concentration camp. I don't know if I'll ever be ready for that. Maybe if I'm with Elvy. If we're there for each other.

"Did you read a travel book or something?" Elvy asks while stealing half my orange. She looks at me, then cracks up. I laugh, too.

"Opa's told me so much, I want to see it for myself. I want to see it with you."

Her innocent look turns to surprise. Her eyes narrow and her nose crinkles a bit, like she's trying to figure out if I've been serious this whole time. When she decides I have been, she smiles.

"Okay, I'll go. But I'm telling you right now, I'm not eating sauerkraut."

"Deal."

CHAPTER 24

Sunday, July 13 – Prince Edward County

"Are you sure this is what you want to do?" Mom asks, before biting the left side of her bottom lip.

We're standing with Alessia and her family outside the sports pub on Main Street. The sidewalks are overflowing, and the air is filled with laughter and conversation and little kid squeals. Picton used to be a sleepy little town, but now it gets all types of tourists coming for wine tours and food tours and art tours, and the beach at Sandbanks, and festivals and shopping. It's almost as busy as Toronto.

"Yeah, Mom. It is," I say, itching to start moving.

She looks at Dad, who nods.

"Okay, we'll be inside if you need us. You come back right after," she says with begging puppy-dog eyes, the worry lines back between her eyebrows.

"I will." I take a step. One step.

"You're sure about this?" She starts biting the right side of her bottom lip. That's new.

"Oh my God," Elvy and I say at the same time.

Alessia's quietly chuckling. In her hand, she's holding a book about soccer. You can't learn soccer from a book, but it's nice of her to try.

Elvy grabs Alessia's other hand and leads her into the pub. I walk the other way. After a couple of minutes, I look over my shoulder. Mom is still watching me.

I keep walking. Away. I reach the light by the Tim Horton's. A delivery truck pulls up beside me. *Farm-fresh poultry* it says in red along the side. I guess the chicken I saw crossing the road was trying to get away from its fate as someone's dinner. One last answer to all those questions I was trying to get away from a month and a half ago. Seems like so much longer.

I cross the street and pass the soldier statue commemorating the two World Wars. There are a lot of names on that statue. I guess because the Trenton air force base isn't too far. I ditch the traffic for a quiet street I've never been on before, passing a plaque about something historic that Dad would make me stop to read if he were here, and reach the cemetery gates. This place is huge, and I have to get to the back. I check out the geese floating and honking in the pond, then shuffle and sprint along one path, and skip onto another. Something moves by my feet, making me freeze. A black and yellow garter snake slithers along the crushed stone path and under some leaves. Wonder who's more afraid of who.

I start walking again. Birds chirp in the tall trees, bees are buzzing around the flowers, there are hills and valleys ... it feels more like a park than a cemetery. Besides all the dead people, I mean. Some stones are so old they're covered in moss or black stuff. Some are etched with flowers, cows, even people's faces, which is kinda creepy. Some last names I recognize from places in the County: the farmer's market, apple-picking, the general store. The funeral home. I stop walking and carefully cross the perfectly mowed grass; we'd never lose an arrow here. I stay a person's length away from the gravestones. I don't want to disturb anyone underneath.

I kneel by the head of Calynn's grave, marked by a couple of flower vases. The sod is as green as artificial soccer turf. It must have been rolled out not too long ago, because I can still see the lines. A Cougars' sweatshirt lies on the sod, over Calynn's body. Her dead body. I shake away the image seared in my brain. It doesn't come as often anymore.

Someone must've put down the sweatshirt this afternoon, because I doubt a cemetery allows stuff like that; it's creepier than those faces.

"Hi Calynn, it's nice to meet you." I take out the pencil flag from the front pocket of my knapsack. The one with Opa's ribbon for bravery. "I think this belongs to you." I push it real deep into the still-soft earth. I pull the snail fossil from my pocket, the one I found on Opa's shore, shine it on my German National jersey. Whenever we visit Zaidie, Mom makes us paint rocks to leave on his gravestone. She says Jews don't bring flowers, we bring rocks because rocks live forever, just like our memories. I put the fossil next to the pencil. I'll bring another when the gravestone is here.

"I wish we could have met for real. I think we would've had lots to talk about." I swing my knapsack over my shoulder. "Thanks for helping Opa. He really liked you."

I walk until I find Opa. He doesn't have a gravestone yet, either, just a casket-length mound of back-filled earth. He also has flowers, and Elvy's stuffed bear. No sweatshirt. I sit down and pull out my laptop. The Black Canadian history book I swiped from Alessia tumbles out with it. I shove it back in, grab my phone, and hotspot the game. I set the laptop on the ground and angle it so we can both see. Opa's under a real old-looking maple that's got to be a hundred feet tall, and it's casting some good shade over him and the screen.

"I guess you want to know who's playing. It's Germany versus Argentina. The final game. Kickoff in two minutes. If Germany wins, it will be the first World Cup they win as a unified country. Yeah, I know they won in 1990. Yeah, I get that the Berlin Wall came down in 1989 and that was the end of the East and West thing. But the 1990 game was played by a *West* German team, and, by the way, they beat Argentina one-nothing back then. Yes, really. No, I didn't learn that in school. Why would I learn that in school? I read it in your book about German soccer. Yeah, yeah, I read a book. Stop laughing."

Good thing he didn't see Alessia's book. He'd be cracking up like that day at the hospital when he got Kane's card. Feels like a lifetime ago. I guess it kind of was.

The whistle blows. I can hear every animated word the announcer says and the excitement and disappointment of the crowd with every level of cheer. No snoring. No gargling. No storytelling. Just the occasional bird chirping and leaves rustling.

"Hey, Opa, I've got a story for you. It starts with a walk down to the lake to find a stone with a fossil ..."

My butt's hurting from sitting on the ground for so long, but my mind is feeling better after talking to Opa. Maybe talking to the therapist would've been helpful. Maybe. I have more important things to think about at the moment: the game's in the second period of extra time with no goals. At this point, the way they've been playing, whichever team scores will win the World Cup. It's been an incredible game. I mean, who doesn't want to watch Lionel Messi and whoever the other Argentinian players are battle the best of Germany. But I don't know. I just don't know.

"They're trying real hard, Opa. They're firing off shots and attacking like crazy, but nothing's going in. Even Messi went wide. I really think it may go into—GOAL!!!" I raise my arms and high-five my nonexistent teammates. I even stand up and do a little dance. Okay, a big dance. No one's watching anyway.

"Götze just scored, Opa! He just scored. He caught the cross with his chest and volleyed it with his left foot right in! Right in! Oh my God. Did you see it, Opa? Did you see it?"

GLOSSARY

German unless otherwise noted

Ach Mensch: Expression meaning "for crying out loud"

Bärchen: Little bear

Brüder: Brothers

Bubbie: Grandmother (Yiddish)

Bundesliga: The German soccer league

Danke: Thank you

Das is gut: That's good

Dokumente: Documents

Entschuldigung: Sorry

Eröffnungsfeier: Opening ceremony

Fotos: photos

Frau: Mrs.

Für: For

Gut: Good

Guten Tag: Good day or hello

Herr: Mr.

Ja: Yes

Ja, natürlich: Yes, of course

Kind: Child

Kinder: Children

Kriegsverdienstkreuz: War merit cross

Mein Prinz: My prince

Mein kleines Mädchen: My little girl

Naja: Anyway

Nein: No

Olympiastadion: Olympic stadium

Oma: Grandmother

Opa: Grandfather

Panzerfaust: Literally, tank fist or tank puncher. Small, handheld anti-tank weapon

Rosinenbomber: Raisin bomber, but refered to in the United States as candy bomber

Uhr: O'clock

Und: And

Vati: Father

Wunderschön: Wonderful

Zaidie: Grandfather (Yiddish)

Zwei: Two

ACKNOWLEDGMENTS

The Other Side would not exist without the stories my father-in-law, Dieter Reppin, recounted, nor would it be so rich in detail without the memoirs my mother-in-law, Elda Nicolai Reppin, and her brother, Aldo Nicolai, wrote for their families. Thank you for sharing your memories.

I am so grateful to:

Marc Reppin for encouraging me to write a novel inspired by his parents' lives, and author/playwright Emil Sher for compelling me to action;

Whale Rock Workshops, especially editor Patricia Lee Gauch for challenging me to go deeper, and author Gary D. Schmidt for keeping me focused and shaping my idea of what children's books are capable of;

Shari Becker, Gary Camlot, Linda Camlot, Elizabeth

Ferguson, Alex Reppin, Juliana Reppin, and Sharlene Wiseman for their input on various drafts, Sanya Dacres for her sensitivity read and feedback, and Gary Taitt for his breadth of soccer knowledge;

Richard Clare for his legal review, Dr. Jonathan Fridell for his medical input, Dr. Sari Fridell for her expertise in clinical, school, and counseling psychology, and Simon Richter for his counsel in criminal law. Any errors are my own;

The Ontario Arts Council for financial assistance, Helena Aalto and CANSCAIP for nonstop encouragement, and the palliative care unit at Sunnybrook Health Sciences Centre for the support they provided my in-laws in their final days;

Finally, Red Deer Press publisher Richard Dionne for his continued support, and editor Peter Carver for his insight, humor, and cheer.

SELECTED SOURCES

"2014 FIFA World Cup Brazil." FIFA.com. Online.

German History from the Middle Ages to the Fall of the Berlin Wall. Permanent Exhibition. 2019. Deutsches Historisches Museum (German Historical Museum), Berlin.

James, Carl. "The crisis of Anti-Black racism in schools persists across generations." TheConversation.com, August 26, 2019. Online.

Käthe Kollwitz: Voice of the People. 13 Oct. 2018 – 3 Mar. 2019, Art Gallery of Ontario, Toronto.

Lyle, D. P. *Forensics: A Guide for Writers.* Cincinnati: Writer's Digest Books. 2008.

Menkis, Richard and Harold Troper. *More Than Just Games: Canada and the 1936 Olympics.* Toronto: University of Toronto Press. 2015.

Permanent Exhibition. 2019. DDR Museum, Berlin.

Permanent Exhibition. 2019. Deutsches Fußballmuseum (German Football Museum), Dortmund.

Vassiltchikov, Marie. *Berlin Diaries, 1940–1945.* New York: Vintage Books. 1988.

Westheimer, Dr. Ruth, quoting from the Talmud: "A lesson taught with humor is a lesson retained." As heard on *The Current.* CBC Radio One. 99.1 Toronto. May 13, 2019.

Art referenced in the novel

Kollwitz, Käthe. "The Survivors," Lithograph, 1923. Toronto: Art Gallery of Ontario.

Kollwitz, Käthe. "Hunger," Woodcut, 1923. Berlin: Deutsches Historiches Museum.

Kollwitz, Käthe. "Visit to the Hospital," Woodcut, 1929. Washington: National Gallery of Art. Online https://www.nga.gov/collection/art-object-page.8203.html

Martchenko, Michael. "McKnight's Hat Trick," Print, 1988. Toronto: Sunnybrook Veterans Centre, Sunnybrook Health Sciences Centre.

Alessia's books

Curtis, Christopher Paul. *Elijah of Buxton.* Toronto: Scholastic Canada. 2007.

Elliott, Zetta. *A Wish After Midnight.* Brooklyn, NY: Rosetta Press. 2008.

Higgins, Dalton. *Far from Over: The Music and Life of Drake.* Toronto: ECW Press. 2012.

Sadlier, Rosemary. *The Kids Book of Black Canadian History.* Toronto: Kids Can Press. 2003.

Wesley, Gloria Ann. *Chasing Freedom.* Black Point, NS: Roseway Publishing. 2011.

INTERVIEW WITH HEATHER CAMLOT

Why did you want to tell this story?

My father-in-law was sixteen when the German army told him he was going to the front, to fight an already lost war. The stories he shared were fascinating and I knew one day I would write about them, but I wasn't sure how. As a Jewish woman, I never heard this side to World War Two: kids given three days of training and a weapon and ordered to fight. But I just couldn't put myself into the body and mind of a German soldier to write historical fiction.

Once I figured out the angle—a grandfather sharing his past with his grandson while together watching the

2014 World Cup—the story came together. As with *Clutch*, I wanted to capture a certain time in history while highlighting other captivating people and stories I discovered through research, like German artist Käthe Kollwitz and Jewish Canadian basketball player Irving "Toots" Meretsky. While writing a novel that I hope will appeal to young readers, I also wanted to give my children a basis to understand their paternal grandparents' history, just as *Clutch* did to an extent for their maternal grandfather. They're personal stories, but I believe they have a universality.

In telling Liam's story, you take the reader into a period of history which, it turns out, has a strong effect on this twelve-year-old boy—even though the historical events took place decades before he was born. Liam discovers that it's just not possible to ignore the past, as Coach suggests. Why was that an important theme for you to explore in telling the story?

The historical events took place decades before I was born too, but I think as we get older we understand we can't escape the past—it's always with us, whether in the shadows or right before our eyes. Whether we see it—or choose to ignore it—is another question. But young people are watching the news on their screens, they know a lot more about what's going on in the world than I think adults give them credit for. They are questioning whether there will be a World War Three and whether their video-game training will help them on the battlefield. I wish I was kidding, but this is the reality.

Meanwhile, we're seeing a rise in anti-Semitism and startling statistics about people young and old not knowing the Holocaust ever happened. If we don't listen to warnings from older generations who lived through these times, if we don't learn about the past, we'll repeat terrible mistakes. We need stories about history, about both "sides" of history, and how there really shouldn't be sides, only humanity. So while Liam doesn't want to listen to Opa's stories at first, he comes to realize he needs to hear them, because even though they happened decades before he was born, they affect his life in the present.

Writers are often given the advice: write what you know. To what extent is that true of your telling the story of Liam and his Opa?

The Other Side was heavily inspired by events I heard, learned, and read about from my husband and his family. I had so many incredible and true stories to work with, but since it's a novel, I fictionalized some, added to others, and made up even more (all backed by research of course).

Obviously, there was no dead body discovered on a beach. And the real Opa wasn't much of a soccer fan, but the rest of us are. I always wonder what and if my kids ever think about being both German and Jewish, the product of two groups with such a horrific history; but Liam's confusion and anger come from my imagination. That said, the real Opa did respond to a letter filled with questions about the war from my son, he did receive the war merit cross for bravery, and some of the stories fictional Opa tells Liam are true, but I won't reveal which ones. There is a lot of real detail in here, including the earwigs in the football and the mouse's crazy death. You can't make that stuff up!

What did you learn about trauma in writing about Liam's discovery of Calynn's body and the host of reactions he suffers in the days and weeks after?

I did a lot of research on distress, trauma, and the impact of seeing a dead body. There are many common psychological, emotional, and physical reactions to trauma, from flashbacks and anxiety to anger and sadness. For Liam's distress—compounded with the looming death of his grandfather, the stories of the past, and the upcoming soccer tryout—I worked with avoidance, distressing dreams, difficulty concentrating, and loss of interest in playing soccer, among others. Liam has a difficult time, but the strong reactions eventually decrease, and his body and mind recover, in part because of the love and support of his family and friends, who don't push him to "get over it."

A story works best when there is a strong cast of supporting characters that provides a contrast to the main character. In this case, Alessia is one of those supporting characters. What do you think she provides to strengthen Liam and his story?
As Liam developed, he needed someone outside of his family whom he could trust, someone who knows him so well he doesn't have to speak to convey what he's thinking or feeling, and of course someone he can joke around with, but also speak seriously with. I think we all need a person like that in our lives. Alessia also provides insight into Opa's stories, offering perspective that Liam doesn't have. I think she is the personification of strength. I'm so glad she spoke up and demanded to be a larger character than just "the friend"—as she was in the first few drafts of the novel.

In writing any story, it can be important for an author to do research so that the characters and events are made more convincing. What can you tell us about the kind of research you had to do in writing *The Other Side*?

I love research! I delve into that rabbit hole of information, whether online or in books, and I don't come out until I find some fascinating gems that I need to share. That was the case with Irving "Toots" Meretsky, the Berlin candy bomber, and the East German escape under slaughtered pigs, among many others.

My mother-in-law and her brother both wrote memoirs for their families, so I studied those, and my husband told me further stories that were handed down throughout the years. I also read autobiographies by Germans who lived through the war, and many how-tos and textbooks about crime scene investigation, child psychology, and criminal law. Fortunately, I live very close to a library.

I also traveled to Germany the summer of 2019. I spent five days in Berlin visiting museums, neighborhoods, the Olympiastadion, the zoo (where I found out about the crocodile soup), and more. Afterwards, I toured parts of the country with my family, a highlight being the city of Dortmund to attend the Borussia Dortmund season opener (they won!) and to visit the German Football Museum. I also watched a lot of 2014 World Cup soccer highlights on my computer. I can't say that was terribly difficult!

Choosing a title is always an interesting part of the job of writing a story. How did you end up with the title for this book?

Interestingly, I had the title when the story was still an idea. A friend one day asked me about what I was working on, then wanted to know what it was called. I said I was toying with *The Other Side*—as in the other side of the war, the other side of the soccer field, the other side of life. I could see him mulling it over ... and then he declared it perfect. From then on, he would ask about *The Other Side*, never "the manuscript" or "the story." It made the novel real—and forced me to get writing.

This is your second novel for young people. What did you discover from writing your first novel, *Clutch*, that helped you with the writing of this one?

The first thing I learned was about voice, having my twelve-year-old characters speak and think like twelve-year-olds. At that time, I was advised to listen to the way my kids talk because that was and is the best reference a writer can have.

The second thing I learned was about using quoted material; each chapter in *Clutch* had a quote about Jackie Robinson and baseball. I really didn't want to go through that process again. But I think the biggest thing I learned is just how much I love writing for young people.

Thank you, Heather, for all your insights—and for your honesty